FIRST SUMMER OUT WITH MY PRISON BAE

ELIJAH R. FREEMAN

URBAN AINT DEAD PRESENTS

URBAN AINT DEAD

P.O Box 448

Maybrook, NY 12543

No part of this book may be reproduced or transmitted in any form by any means electronic or mechanical, including photocopying, recording, or by any information storage system, without written permission from the publisher.

Copyright © 2025 By Elijah R. Freeman

All rights reserved. Published by URBAN AINT DEAD Publications.

Cover Design: P. Wise / The Wise Services

Edited By: Shawna Brim / Ladies of Lit

URBAN AINT DEAD and coinciding logo(s) are registered properties.

No patent liability is assumed with respect to the use of information contained herein. Although every precaution has been taken in the preparation of this book, the publisher and the author assume no responsibility for errors or omissions. Neither is any liability assumed for damages resulting from the use of the information contained herein. This is a work of fiction. Names, characters, places, and incidents are either the product of the author's imagination or are used fictitiously. Any resemblance to actual events, locales, or persons living or dead is entirely coincidental.

Contact Author on FB: Elijah R. Freeman / IG: @the_future_of_urban_-fiction

Contact Publisher at www.urbanaintdead.com

Email: urbanaintdead@gmail.com

Print ISBN: 979-8-218-74267-6

STAY UP TO DATE

To stay up to date on new releases, plus get information on contests, sneak peeks and more,

Click the link below...
https://mailchi.mp/6d21003686d1/subscribe

Scan the QR Code below to listen to the Soundtracks/Singles
of some of your favorite U.A.D titles:

Don't have Spotify or Apple Music?
No Sweat!
Visit your choice streaming platform and search URBAN
AINT DEAD.

Currently on lock serving a bid?
JPay, iHeartRadio, WHATEVER!

We got you covered.
Simply log into your facility's kiosk or tablet, go to music
and search URBAN AINT DEAD.

U.A.D PRESENTS

Like & Follow us on social media:

FB - URBAN AINT DEAD

IG: @uadpresents

Tik Tok - @uadpresents

.

Submission Guidelines

Submit the first three chapters of your completed manuscript to urbanaintdead@gmail.com, subject line: Your book's title. The manuscript must be in a .doc file and sent as an attachment. The document should be in Times New Roman, double-spaced, and in size 12 font. Also, provide your synopsis and full contact information. If sending multiple submissions, they must each be in a separate email. Have a story but no way to submit it electronically? You can still submit to URBAN AINT DEAD. Send in the first three chapters, written or typed, of your completed manuscript to:

URBAN AINT DEAD
P.O Box 448
Maybrook, NY 12543

DO NOT send original manuscript. Must be a duplicate.
Provide your synopsis and a cover letter containing your full contact information.
Thanks for considering URBAN AINT DEAD.

CHAPTER ONE

Dominique breathed a sigh of relief as she stepped over the threshold and into her beautiful townhome after completing a twelve-hour shift at Telfair State Prison. Though the day had been long, it had been a relatively easy one. There were no major incidents, so the day wasn't all that eventful.

She had just placed her work bag on the table beside the front door and put her keys in the glass bowl that rested on top of it when a familiar ring signaling that she was receiving a video call filled the air of the almost too quiet home.

Dominique answered the phone. "Look at you, always so in tune with me. You were just on my mind," she cooed. A sweet smile pulled at her full lips as she gazed lovingly into the camera. Ramello folded a piece of paper the long way and put it in his cell door window to keep inmates and officers from seeing into his cell when they passed by. Jamming the door, he walked to the bottom bunk, and stretched his six-foot-two frame out across his cot, his athletic frame enticing her like no other.

"Oh, yeah? And what exactly was going on in that pretty little head of yours?" The sound of Ramello's deep baritone voice was like music to her ears. In fact, it was easily one of her favorite sounds, second only to the sound of his moans in her ear when they made love.

Mentally, Dominique was making heart eyes at her man as she made her way to her bedroom. Ramello, a man that she had made a fated connection with while working as a nurse at Valdosta State Prison just over a year prior, was lounging on his cot, making heart eyes right back at her. They stared at one another as a few moments of silence went by, both of them taking one another in.

Connecting.

Both of them feeling grateful to be basking in one another's ambience.

"How much I missed you." She blew him a kiss. Whenever she was on the phone with him, her voice had a tendency of softening and raising a couple of octaves. Hell, her whole body responded to him every time that they spoke.

Her shoulders relaxed.

Heart melted.

And pussy pulsed with need each time she gazed into his handsome face.

"And *my* dick," she added seductively at the end. A mischievous grin spread across her delicate features that made her brown, almond-shaped eyes narrow into slits.

The tip of Dominique's tongue darted out to seductively swipe across her top lip, a subconscious reaction to her taking in the sight of her shirtless man, before she bit into her bottom one. His state issued boxers and pants hung low on his hips. A tent beginning to spring up in his pants only enticed her even more. His hair had been freshly lined up, and his waves were swimming. He knew what the fuck he was doing.

"Now, why you wanna tease me like that?" she asked and pretended to lick him. "Just fine as fuck for no reason." She shook her head, accompanied by a moan.

A deep chuckle rumbled through Ramello's chest as his top teeth sank into his bottom lip, biting back a grin. The naughty nurse never failed to stroke his ego and make him feel wanted and desired. It was part of what made him addicted to her and her love. In a place where he lived in hell, Dominique had become his slice of heaven on earth. He thanked Allah daily for placing her along his path in this lifetime. She made him feel like a king.

"I'm so in tune because you belong to me. I be all in yo head, Mama. Remember that." Ramello smirked as he watched Dominique grab the tripod that he had bought her from her nightstand and begin making her way to her attached bathroom.

She knew exactly why he had called and was already preparing to give her man exactly what she knew he wanted.

"Mhm," she hummed with a smirk as she fumbled with the phone and tripod, placing it on the countertop of the sink beside the walk-in shower of her bathroom. "What do I owe the pleasure of being able to hear your voice?" she asked.

"Nun major. A nigga just wanted to see yo fine ass naked while you showered," Ramello said.

He casually laid back, one hand behind his head, the other trailing down his abdomen to grip his hard dick through his pants. Once Dominique was satisfied with the angle that she had set up for her man, she turned on the shower then began stripping out of her scrubs. Ramello watched as his woman peeled her top off, exposing the black lace bra that she wore underneath. His eyes were low with lust watching her turn around and seductively bend over as she removed her scrub bottoms, revealing a pair of matching lace panties. Her mahogany skin was soft and made him wish that he could reach through the phone and caress her.

"Damn, I miss being inside of you," Ramello said with a shake of his head.

Dominique had turned to face him again, stripping out of her bra and panties. Ramello's dick grew even harder at the sight of her dark areolas and erect nipples staring at him. He admired her thickness. She wasn't shy about her round belly. With the confidence she possessed, you had no choice but to love her.

A half smile tugged at the corner of his lips when, as if almost reading his mind, his woman turned around and bent over once more, this time using her dainty hands to spread her big ass cheeks, exposing both of her pretty holes.

"Fuck…" Ramello groaned and pulled his throbbing dick from his pants.

"I miss feeling that big ass dick inside of this pussy too, Daddy," Dominique cooed. She reached a hand between her thick thighs and spread her pussy lips for him.

Ramello fisted his dick to the image of her pink walls while recalling how good she felt wrapped around his length. It had been six long months since the couple had been able to be intimate. The couple first met at his previous camp, Valdosta State Prison, when he was rushed to the nurse's office after being stabbed during a fight. The chemistry between the two had been instant, neither of them able to resist the sexual attraction that was evidently there. What had started out as a naughty fling between an inmate and a prison nurse had turned into something deeper than either of them could have imagined.

A few of what they thought were lowkey rendezvous had drawn unnecessary attention to them, causing a member of the GDs named Knowledge to come knocking on Ramello's prison door. He accused Ramello of sleeping with his woman, Sierra — who not only worked at the prison as a corrections officer but was also Dominique's best friend. Ramello knew Knowledge well enough to understand that, despite his name, the man lacked common sense and posed a threat — not just to him but to Dominique and her job as well. Determined to protect them, Ramello pulled some strings, made a few moves, and had him dealt with.

Knowledge had been found dead in his cell with his throat slit. The hit should have been the end to all of their drama, but shortly after, they had brought even more heat on themselves. It didn't take long for the GDs to catch on to the nature of Ramello's relationship with the nurse and put two and two together.

They wanted smoke for Knowledge's death.

Three months after the slaying of Knowledge, Ramello had got wind of the GDs putting a hit on him, so he set his own plan in motion. He devised a plan to get Looney G — the head GD at the time — out of the dorm and away from any potential help. Using Looney's name, he put a sick call in the medical box, claiming Looney needed to be seen for chest pains. It was the perfect setup. To ensure the plan went smoothly, Ramello and several of his Muslim brothers also submitted sick calls under their own names, ensuring they would all be called to medical on the same day.

When the day came, Looney arrived at the medical unit, waiting in the bullpen to be seen. Unbeknownst to him, Ramello and his brothers were already there, lying in wait. They ambushed him in the bullpen, stabbing him repeatedly in a calculated attack. The injuries were so severe that Looney had to be airlifted by helicopter to a hospital outside the prison, barely clinging to life. In the aftermath, Ramello and the other Muslims involved were immediately separated and transferred to different facilities as an emergency measure. Once Ramello was relocated, Dominique decided to quit her job at Valdosta. Three months later, she followed him to his new location.

The nursing office at the new camp was larger than the one at Valdosta. A bigger office meant there were more people to fill it. Dominique had gone from working solo to now having a partner who she worked with day to day. It was the main reason she and Ramello hadn't been able to get it in in the last six months they'd been there. Dominique's co-worker, Renee, was a square.

She did things by the books and had a tendency for running her mouth about things that had nothing to do with her. Having watched her in action, Dominique let Ramello know that Renee was too much of a hazard to attempt anything. So, they settled for knowing that one another was still close by and cherished the fleeting moments that they saw each other in passing.

Ramello put a pillow behind him to prop himself up a bit, the bright florescent light of the cell beaming above. He wanted to make sure Dominique could see that dick when he came for her. The walls around him were cold, gray, and unforgiving, but the sight on his screen was the only warmth he needed. Dominique's naked body filled his view, glistening under the soft light of her bathroom, every curve accentuated by the steam rising from her shower. His breathing grew heavier as he adjusted the phone in one hand, his other hand gliding slowly along his eight-inch length of chocolate, savoring the moment while she teased him through the screen.

"Yeah?" His voice was low, thick with longing, barely above a whisper so as not to catch the attention of the guards patrolling outside his cell. "You miss this dick, Dominique?"

Her whimper broke through the speaker, soft yet intoxicating. "I do, baby… I miss it so fuckin' much." She slapped her ass, shaking it for him, a playful taunt that made him stroke faster.

"Get yo fine ass in the shower and show me den," he ordered, his tone rough, raw with desire.

"Okay, Mr. Impatient. Hold on." She giggled, sliding open the shower door and stepping inside.

Watching her shower had become one of Ramello's favorite pastimes. He loved the way she turned a daily to-do into something so sensual. Having been locked up so long, little shit turned him on. And Dominique caught onto that quickly.

For a few seconds, the screen went blurry as she adjusted her phone's position, propping it on the bathroom counter. When it refocused, Ramello's heart nearly leaped out of his chest. Dominique glistened as streams of water cascaded down her body and soap suds slid along her curves with agonizing slowness. He groaned lightly, stroking himself harder now, wishing that his hand was hers instead.

"Uh huh," he murmured as Dominique squeezed her loofa between her breasts, pushing them together and jiggling them at him. She was putting on a hell of a show tonight, and he couldn't look away. Even in the chill of his cell, sweat broke across his brow, his body warming with every move she made.

She turned her back to the camera and jumped, making her ass clap. Ramello's jaw slackened slightly at the unexpected move, his strokes slowing as he stared in disbelief.

"Oou, you showin' out for me tonight?" he asked, his voice dropping an octave.

"You know I'ma always show out for you, Daddy," Dominique purred, glancing over her shoulder at the camera with a smile that could undo him entirely.

"You promise?" His voice trembled as his need for her hit its peak.

"I promise, baby." Dominique turned back toward the camera, her smirk never faltering. She lifted a leg, planting it on the built-in soap dish, and spread herself open for him, her fingers sliding between her folds. She moaned softly, the sound coming through the speaker like music meant only for his ears.

Ramello licked his lips, sweat dampening his hairline, his strokes becoming sloppy as he fell deeper under her spell. "You love me?" His voice cracked as he got closer to his release, teetering on the edge.

Dominique's moans intensified, her fingers working faster. "Yes," she breathed heavily, her words spilling out between gasps. "I love you so much, Ramello."

The moment his name left her lips, Ramello's entire body seized as he released himself, the tension finally breaking, his soft curses of pleasure barely audible. For a minute, he slouched back against the wall, the screen still glowing in his hands.

"Mmm," Dominique moaned and blew a series of kisses at him. "I love it when you cum for me."

"And I love to cum for yo freaky ass," he replied with a chuckle, while he cleaned his mess up with a rag.

Dominique giggled and finished her shower.

"How was yo day, sexy?" Ramello asked after he finished cleaning. His arms were behind his head, watching Dominique and enjoying the view.

"It was fine, nothing too crazy. A couple of toothaches, a strep throat, and then the usual diabetics."

Ramello nodded. "Was yo homegirl being cool?"

Dominique stepped out of the shower and side-eyed him, making him chuckle at her irritation. She hated when he referred to Renee as that. "Now you know good and damn well that lady ain't my homegirl."

"Yeah, she is. She tryna take Sierra's place in a minute," he continued to tease.

Dominique snorted. "You get on my damn nerves. And speaking of homegirls, I talked to your mama today, and she wants to throw you a coming home party the day you get out." She changed the subject.

She and Ramello's mother had gotten close over the last few months since he had given his mom her contact information in case anything happened to him, considering their circumstances at the time. His mother had taken the opportunity to get to know the woman her son was risking his life for.

"Aw, hell nah." He waved a hand dismissively in the air. "I don't wanna be 'round a bunch of people when I get out. I'm just tryna be in some pussy."

She laughed at his response as she dried her body with a fluffy white towel. "We'll have the rest of our lives to do that, baby. Plus, it's better to get it over with, so we ain't gotta rush. We'll finally be able to take our time, Daddy. That alone will be worth the wait."

Ramello smiled through the camera. He appreciated that she was always so considerate. "You gotta point there, my love."

"And stop actin like you don't miss yo folks. It's been a long time," she added, throwing her soiled towel and scrubs into the dirty clothes hamper before proceeding to the sink to brush her teeth.

"Aight now…" Ramello smirked at her, his words a light warning.

She had made her point.

Dominique slightly rolled her eyes but said nothing and finished brushing her teeth before she changed the subject again. "On another note, I got something special planned for you after we leave your mom's."

"Mhmm. I bet. You need anything?"

"For?"

"Whatever you got planned."

Dominique's face went blank. "Bae, what I look like

spending your money on you? No, I don't need anything. But I appreciate you offering. Can I have a kiss?"

Ramello laughed and kissed her through the phone. "My bad, bae. I ain't tryin' you. You know how I am."

And she did. He made it so that she didn't want for anything. Dominique's needs were often met before she even expressed them. A few months ago, he had her set up an account in her name that he funded. Being the solid nigga he was, he made sure that an influx of money touched each one of her accounts. He had her open an account specifically for emergencies and a brokerage account, so she could invest in stocks and Bitcoin.

Dominique wanted for nothing and never had Ramello complained about providing for her. She loved the fuck out of him for it. It was because of him that she knew what it meant to truly be secure in a relationship.

"Thank youuu," she sang as she grabbed the tripod and pranced into her bedroom where she set him up on her nightstand. "I'ma send ya mama some money for the party too. That cool?"

"Mhmm…" Ramello hummed, too busy loving the show. She had grabbed her body oil, and he knew what was coming next. "Rub that oil on that booty for Daddy, baby."

Dominique laughed. "Bae, focus!"

"Oh, yeah. Do that for me and what you plannin' for us?"

"It's a surprise." She smirked. Her fingers methodically caressed her body as she moisturized every part of her soft skin.

"Booo." He put two thumbs down, his eyes following every movement of her hands on her body.

The intensity of his stare, even through a camera, scorched her skin, setting every part of her ablaze.

Dominique laughed. "Shut up."

That was one of her favorite things about Ramello. He

always kept her smiling and laughing, and he did it so effortlessly. She couldn't remember doing either as much as she had been since she had met him. He genuinely made her happy. She never wanted to go back to the dull life that she had before she met him.

Ramello only smiled at her. His eyes were getting heavy thanks to the nut he had busted just moments earlier.

Once she had completely oiled her body and moisturized her face, she crawled in between her silk sheets and settled into bed. With her stomach full from the chicken sandwich combo she'd picked up from Popeyes on the way home and ate in the car, she was content for the night.

"Nine more days, baby… nine more days…" Dominique mumbled after a minute.

They were both dozing off, both of their eyes repeatedly closing and opening to see if the other had fallen asleep yet, but neither of them attempted to end the call.

"And I can't fuckin' wait…" were the last words spoken before they both drifted off into a deep sleep.

THE NEXT DAY, Dominique found herself lounging around her place, dressed in her silk, pink pajamas. Today, like most of her off days, was spent in her living room, binge watching *Master Chef*.

The green, cream, and grey color scheme of the living room décor was unique to her. There were a total of three couches in the living room space: a cream, double loveseat, a gray recliner, and green sofa.

Each wall of the living room was painted one of the three colors. She loved to mix and match and color block things. Potted plants and flowers overflowed the space, making it seem as if it was almost built for a fairy.

A square glass table stood at the center of the room, its surface adorned with a tiny fountain. The gentle trickle of water echoed softly, its soothing sound calming her spirit.

Her place reflected her personality.

Her iPhone was tucked between her shoulder and her ear as she chatted on the phone with her best friend since childhood.

"Eight more days and my baby is gonna be home." A tinkling laugh escaped her lips, her head falling back with joy.

"They finally finna free that nigga, huh?" Sierra asked.

"Yeaaah." She let out a content sigh. "And I can't fuckin' wait."

"Mhm," Sierra responded dryly.

"Speaking of which, I need to look around and see what we're gonna do after we leave his coming home party that night." Mentioning Ramello made her remember that she was supposed to start planning for his first day out.

She reached across the couch to grab her laptop from the other end, bringing it within easy reach.

Just after 1:30 p.m., she'd spent the morning discussing plans with Shantae, Ramello's mother, for his upcoming homecoming party. After sending Shantae $2,000 via Cash App, they collaborated to create a list of everything needed to ensure the evening would be special for their favorite person.

Knowing this would be her only day off before working the entire week leading up to Ramello's release, she made it a priority to handle everything that needed attention. It had already been established that once her man was out, there'd be no reason for her to continue working at the prison. So, she planned to make the most of her time as a prison nurse, finish her final duties, and walk away once Ramello was free.

Sierra sucked her teeth. "Why I didn't get an invite?"

Dominique's eyebrows pulled together. "Cause he don't

know you. The fuck?" She lightened the blow with a laugh at the end. She hated when Sierra started with that clingy shit.

Having been best friends since the first grade, they had shared countless ups and downs over the years. Knowing someone for more than two decades meant witnessing all their seasons — seeing their light, their shadows, and even meeting their demons.

Sierra was the friend Dominique had known the longest, and because of their history and secrets kept between one another, Sierra felt that Dominique owed her unwavering loyalty.

"That nigga ain't know me when he had me takin' him to fuck you!" Sierra sneered.

Dominique downed the rest of her mimosa in two big gulps. "Yeah, I'ma hang up before I cuss yo ass out."

Sierra laughed once. "That nigga got you actin' different. You even startin' to sound like his ass."

Dominique's face twisted in disbelief as a surge of anger began to simmer in her chest. "And?" Her neck swung in a circle. "Do I say anything when you get to actin' funny when you around them bum ass niggas you fuck with? No! So don't say shit bout the solid nigga I'm with."

The line went silent for a minute.

Dominique rolled her eyes, annoyed at her friend for making her tweak out. Sierra knew she struck a nerve. When it came to her man, Dominique was ten toes down. No questions asked.

"I can't believe you just said that…"

Dominique groaned out loud and put her wine glass on the glass table. "Now I'm wrong 'cause you tellin' me *I'm* actin funny. Ha!"

"Shit, you ain't never cussed me out 'bout no nigga before…"

"I never cared as much before. This one, I'm gon' go to

hell about every time," Dominique said. She sat back and pulled her laptop into her lap. *I'm not stuntin' this bitch,* she thought to herself as she opened the device and launched her Chrome browser, typing "what are some fun date night activities in Atlanta?" in the search bar.

There was nothing that Sierra or *anyone* could say about Ramello to change how she felt about him.

"See! Brainwashed! That shit don't even *sound* like you, Dominique! You've changed!" Sierra let out a sob.

Dominique put a hand on her forehead in confusion. *What is she crying for?* "Sierra, why are you crying right now? You're mad because I've changed? That's what we're supposed to do! Everybody is supposed to change."

Sierra sobbed on the other side of the phone, not saying anything.

Annoyed, Dominique spoke again. "Okay, you can cry by your damn self. You trippin'."

Click. She didn't give her the chance to respond.

Got me on the phone arguing with her like she's my bitch or somethin'. Dominique sighed and shook her head. This hadn't been the first time that Sierra pulled theatrics; it was something that she liked to do whenever she felt like she was "losing" her best friend to someone else.

Even in the last couple of relationships that Dominique had, a major part of them ending was because of Sierra, her clinginess, and her constantly pulling Dominique into drama. In the end, it always came down to a "Sierra or them" ultimatum, and because she was extremely loyal, she always chose Sierra. They had entirely too much history to throw away over a man that she had no real feelings for.

Ramello was different though…

Dominique had long since made up her mind that she wouldn't allow Sierra to ruin what she had with him. She was fully prepared to drop Sierra as a friend if it came down to it.

Though Dominique loved Sierra, she was ready to settle down, love, be loved on, and have a few babies of her own. Because things had not worked out for Sierra or any of her baby daddies, she had a predisposition about men, thinking that there were no true good men out there.

Sierra had three children with two different men, but she had lost custody of all of them. Each child now lived with their respective father. From Sierra's perspective, she believed she had been wronged, convinced that the system was stacked against her. However, the reality was that her pattern of bringing a revolving door of random men into her home was something the fathers couldn't tolerate, prompting them to take action to secure a better environment for their children. Two of her three kids were girls. Simply put, Sierra's habits were a danger and detriment to them, and her baby daddies did the right thing by taking her to court. Once a month, she was able to have supervised visits.

Sierra acted like it deeply bothered her that she didn't have custody of her children, but she didn't really give a fuck. In fact, it bothered Dominique *more* that her best friend didn't have her kids, but she didn't bring it up often because she knew they were better off with their fathers. They had become an off-limits topic shortly after Sierra lost them four years prior. All that came of it was a messy argument and hurt feelings.

The entire situation was another reason why Dominique wouldn't hesitate to cut Sierra off if it came down to it. She was stuck in toxic and negative loops that were doing nothing but setting her back in life, and she refused to allow Sierra to drag her down with her.

If that meant she was going to be called fake and disloyal for it, then that was what it was going to be. She'd get over it. After finally reaching a point in life where she literally had nothing to worry about, she absolutely refused to allow Sierra to fuck up a good thing for her.

Dominique let out an exasperated sigh, curled up on her couch, and continued googling things she and Ramello could do upon his release. She ignored her ringing phone when Sierra tried calling her back a few minutes later.

"What should we do?" Dominique inhaled deep and released a heavy sigh as she scrolled through a blog post titled *50 Fun Things To Do In Atlanta.*

I can't see Ramello wanting to do any of this, she thought.

From museums, art centers, film studios, and botanical gardens, none of it seemed to match Ramello's swag and taste, nor were they flashy enough. Dominique felt that her man deserved some top-notch shit.

Closing her laptop, Dominique took a moment to think about what kind of things *would* match Ramello's vibe.

She let her eyes flutter closed, exhaling into a soft smile as her thoughts sank into something sweeter, warmer, wetter — about what she would enjoy doing with Ramello once he was finally freed from the gates of hell that they called prison and was back in her arms. Dominique rested her back against the soft cushions of the loveseat and allowed her body to fully relax as she engaged her imagination and all of her senses.

Slowly, the vision became clear, and a smile tugged at her lips as she saw it all…

What they did.

What they wore.

What they expressed.

What they *felt.*

Yeah… he's gonna love this shit!

Dominique sat up and opened her laptop again, her fingers tapping away at the keyboard as she began making bookings right away.

CHAPTER TWO

LATER THAT DAY, Dominique had just finished unloading her car and setting down the last of the shopping bags when her phone rang, signaling an incoming video call. She smiled, reaching into the left side of her bra to retrieve her phone, already knowing exactly who it would be.

"How is it that you always know *right* when I make it in the house, bae?" she asked, amusement in her voice.

Ramello smirked. "Come on now. You know I'm trackin' that ass."

"No." She giggled. "I didn't know that."

"Shiiid." Ramello scratched at the stubble on his cheek. "Since that lil shit back at Valdosta popped off, a nigga just been wantin' to make sure my baby make it home safe. How was yo shoppin' though?"

Dominique nodded but said nothing. Ramello tracking her had never crossed her mind. She knew he was big on protecting her. That was evident in the way he moved daily. She had left what happened at Valdosta there and hadn't considered it following them home. Dominique didn't know just how serious prison politics could get. To know that he took the extra precautionary measure made her feel safe.

Ramello deemed it necessary until he made it home.

"Shopping was fine. I was able to find most of what I was looking for. A few other things I wanna get you, I'll have to get online, but other than that, we're all set, Daddy." She walked to the kitchen to take out the ground beef that she planned on using to make herself tacos for the night.

"Fasho. What you makin' us tonight?" Ramello asked.

"Tacos!" Dominique grinned into the camera as she continued pulling out ingredients she would need for her food.

He chuckled. "Of course you are." They were her favorite.

She propped her phone up on a countertop and used a bottle of salt to hold it up. "Mhmm, how was your day?"

"Regular. Ain't much goin' on, baby. Just what I want till they free me up out this bitch!" He lay on his side, propped up on one forearm. A black skully cap hugged his head, pulled low over his thick eyebrows.

"Alhamdulillah! Alhamdulillah! Alhamdulillah!" Dominique shouted and began to praise dance.

Ramello burst out laughing at her reply. It was a true laugh, one that came from deep down. No one knew how to make him laugh the way she did.

He also loved when she made efforts to relate to him when it came to his religion. She wasn't much of a religious woman, but she did enjoy talking about the subject of it and often expressed interest in learning about his. It always warmed his heart and made him feel good when she took the opportunity to flex her newfound knowledge when it came to Islam, thanks to him.

The woman had game and knew just how to bag him. He fell for her deeper and deeper with each day that passed. Her actions always proved that she felt the same.

"You is crazy, girl," he said once his laughter died down. "I called to talk to you though…"

Dominique, who had been facing away from him, turned, stepped forward, picked the phone up, and looked at the screen before leaning against the countertop. Noticing the seriousness in his tone, she was curious about what was on his mind. "W'sup, baby?"

He turned and laid on his back. "I just been thinkin' about what's gonna come after this… once I'm out…" He turned his head to look at Dominique and gauge her reaction.

"I'm listening, Melly." She gently encouraged him to continue, her face soft and receptive.

His face relaxed. He could feel it in his eyebrows, the pressure that he hadn't noticed was there subsiding. It seemed like the closer he got to his release date, the more anxious he became as well. He wasn't quite sure why, as he couldn't *wait* to leave, but he didn't want to entertain the emotion too long. Instead, he opted to push it down and focus on his woman.

"You okay?" Dominique asked after a minute of silence. That wasn't like him.

"Yeah… Yeah, I'm good, baby. I just… I been thinking about what comes after all this, ya know?" He did his best to communicate what he had yet to be able to find words for.

He had his whole future ahead of him, and he had to make a lot of decisions as to how he was going to spend it. Dominique was part of him *and* his future. So, the talk that they were getting ready to have was necessary.

Dominique's face softened as she opened herself up for whatever it was that he wanted to discuss. She held her tongue, allowing him to take his time.

"There's something we need to talk about but haven't yet. I been rackin' my brain tryna figure out how to bring it up, and I feel like now is as great a time as ever."

Dominique nodded yet remained quiet and resumed with

her cooking, making sure to nod and give him eye contact every once in a while to let him know she was still listening.

"First things first, I need to figure out where I'ma stay. I can stay with my momma…"

"Well, you know you ain't got to stay at your momma's house," Dominique interrupted him.

Ramello smiled at her interruption but continued on as if she hadn't said anything. "But I ain't really tryna do that. And I know you have no problem with me coming and staying with you. That was my original plan anyway, but I didn't want to assume in case you had somethin' else in mind. I would only stay with you until I find us a new place, then we can move together and sell or rent your townhouse. Whatever you want to do, baby."

Dominique had moved the phone from on the countertop to a different countertop next to the stove where she was putting her ground beef into a pan. She thought about what he said for a moment before responding in a soft voice. "I don't have any objections to that plan."

He nodded, trying to hold back a smile. "Okay, cool. That solves that. You already put your two week notice in, right?"

Dominique nodded again. "Yep, my last day is the day before your release on the twelfth."

"Good. Good. The next thing I wanted to halla at you 'bout was yo homegirl." He sounded annoyed the moment he mentioned her. "I don't really care to have her 'round me like that. So, all that her comin' over and chillin' shit is out. You feel me?"

"I hear you." Dominique sighed.

"But do you *feel* me though?"

"I *feel* you, Ramello… I'm just… frustrated. I understand exactly what you're saying. I got into it with her ass today anyway. She was talking about you got me brainwashed and that I'm acting funny and different and whatever the hell else she was talking about." She used one hand to stir the meat in her pan and the other one went in the air with an exasperated sigh. "She always does this shit when she feels like she's about to lose me as a friend."

"I'm telling you that ho is jealous of you. She mad you got a good man that takes care of you and wants you to be miserable just like her ass. Don't let her get in the way of your happiness, Mini," Ramello reasoned with her.

Dominique silently continued cooking.

"I already told myself that if she kept on with the bullshit that I would cut her off. I'm at a point in my life where I'm requiring everyone around me to be growing and leveling up. If you ain't on that type of timing, then you just can't be around me. It's that simple. People are either going to rise to the occasion or they're going to get left where they're at. Period." She shrugged dismissively.

Ramello's mindset had really rubbed off on her.

She was trying to play it off like she was cool, but it was deeply bothering her that the reality was she knew Sierra wouldn't be able to meet her new standards. She didn't want to change, therefore she wouldn't. Dominique wasn't going to beg her to in order to keep her in her life. However it ended up playing out was just what it was going to have to be.

Ramello's face lit up with pride. "I like that answer."

Dominique let out a tinkling laugh. "I know you do."

"Now, tell me what led up to her calling you brainwashed."

Dominique went on to recount the conversation that she had with Sierra earlier in the day.

"How she gon' be mad you tryna plan somethin' nice for yo nigga? That's a blatant sign right there that she jealous."

"I mean…" Dominique took a deep breath. "Fuck it. I'ma just say it… She's been acting like this since the first time I let her eat my pussy when we were teenagers, okay? Yes, I know she's jealous, but she's not jealous in the way that you think. Sierra has always wanted to be my girlfriend, but I have never wanted to be more than just friends with her. Yes, we fuck from time to time, but she has it made up in her mind that I will one day change my mind, and we'll be together.

"She even says that she's okay with the two of us messing around from time to time, but it ain't like we do that often anyway. The last time I did something with her was back when we had that threesome with you a year ago," Dominique blurted out.

Ramello remained quiet for a few minutes.

"I don't even know what to say to that to be honest. I ain't know it was that deep," Ramello replied nonchalantly.

"It's *not* that deep at all actually. She ate my pussy. I ate hers. We bump coochies for a little bit. Then, once we're done, we go right back to being best friends. She wants more. I don't. She can't *force* me to do shit." Dominique shrugged.

"So, how are you going to solve the problem then?" Ramello's eyebrows creased in irritation.

"Tell her to get her shit together or we can no longer be friends." She couldn't hide the attitude that seeped into her words. He was making it more complicated than it needed to be.

"Do you really think she gon' be able to do that?" Ramello replied, doubt evident in his voice. His expression was blank.

Dominique began chopping up some red and green bell peppers for her tacos. "I don't actually, but I'm going to give her an opportunity to prove me wrong."

"Sounds to me like you just want to waste time." Ramello's tone was curt.

"Look, I've known this girl since first grade, and she's been there with me through *everything*. That's over twenty years, Ramello. The least I can do is allow her to try to prove me wrong. Have you ever had to cut off somebody that you've known for over twenty years?"

Ramello didn't say anything.

"If I want to waste time in this instance, allow me to do that. Please? You and I both already know that you're gonna win in this situation, so…"

He wanted to argue, but he chose to let it go. He understood that what she was being asked wouldn't be easy. When someone had been a part of your life for so long, standing by you through some of your toughest moments, letting them go was no simple task. What he heard was that she needed time to end things with her best friend — and he was willing to give her that.

All he knew was that it better happen.

"Aight, next subject… You ready for me to put a baby or three in you?" he asked with a smirk. He needed to lighten the subject.

Dominique burst out laughing at his antics. "I'll be ready to give you all the babies you want after we've enjoyed some time with each other first. Don't you want to get to know me a little more before you start putting babies in me? What if I turned out to be a crazy baby mama?"

"That ain't nothin' I don't know how to handle," he countered, his dick hardening at the turn of their conversation. The thought of her belly swollen with his seed turned him on. "You're right about getting to know you more, but I've seen enough. I'm willing to deal with whatever comes with you."

Dominique bit her lip, aroused by his confidence. She turned around and began to twerk. "Then come on with it, sir."

"Aight, you better chill out…" Ramello warned, gripping his crotch with desire.

"I'ma chill. I'ma chill. I wanna get these tacos done. I ain't trying to get you worked up." Dominique giggled.

"Uh-huh. I can't wait to touchdown and work *you* out. All. Mufuckin'. Night. Long." He shook his head, looking her up and down. "I really miss feeling you wrapped around this dick."

"Ugh, I miss it more. We're almost there, baby. Almost there," Dominique said dreamily.

<hr>

IT WAS the night before Ramello was released, and he lay on his cot, anxious and excited all at the same time. He was hours away from freedom, and he doubted he was going to be getting any sleep that night. Not that it mattered anyway. He was going to get plenty of sleep once he was released. And the best part about it was that he was going to be able to do so *peacefully*. His mind was racing, thinking about all the lost time that he had to make up for in almost every area of his life. He had family and friends that he was excited to see and catch up with. Exploring the city of Atlanta again and seeing how much had changed in the seven years he had been caged up was something that he was looking forward to doing as well. But most of all, he was looking forward to creating a new life with Dominique, a blessing that had come completely out of left field but that he was grateful for in every sense of the word. He had never expected to align with her along his path, but some way, somehow, she had decided that he was worth entertaining and getting to know even though he was a convicted felon *in* prison when she met him.

A couple of months into them dating and getting to know each other, Dominique had admitted to him that messing with inmates was something that she was completely against before she met him.

"It's funny because I've never been attracted to any of the inmates that came down to the office before you."

Ramello sucked his teeth. "Maaan, you so cap. Yeen gotta do all that."

"No, I'm serious. Were some of them attractive? Of course. But like... actually being attracted to any of them? Nah. None of them were worth risking my license for." Dominique was laying naked in her bed after they had an intimate session. She was laying on her side, her blanket pulled over the bottom half of her body and her breasts spilling over the top.

Ramello's mouth twisted to the side in disbelief. "So, you ain't never fucked wit' no inmate before?"

"No." Dominique laughed at his facial expression.

"Nah, I don't believe you." He chuckled. He was laying on his cot in a white wife beater with one hand behind his head. "You were too comfortable jackin' my dick the first time you met me to not have done it before."

Dominique shrugged one shoulder. "Fair enough. Still doesn't change the fact that it's the truth... I don't know, Melly baby... It's just always been something about you that brings out my inner ho. That day, all I know is that I wanted to please you."

She bit her lip, and her long mascara coated eyelashes fluttered in remembrance.

Ramello's dick jumped. He was also reminiscing on the first time he felt her hands wrapped around his length. It was the first touch from a woman he had felt in six long years. He nutted hard as fuck that day.

"I can't wait to bring her out every night once I'm home." His imagination was running wild.

"Every night, huh? You think you gonna be able to keep up with that?" Dominique teased.

Ramello scoffed at her words. "Girl, I been locked up with no pussy for years. I'm beatin' that pussy up every night to make up for lost time. Fuck you thought?"

His words came from a lustful space.

Dominique moaned out loud. "Don't threaten me with a good time."

"So, you really ain't been with another nigga in prison before?" he asked a final time.

"No. I was actually really anti about it. Sierra had been trying to convince me to do it for a while, but I just never cared to get involved. Especially since she was doing it. She doesn't make the best decisions. So, I figured it was only a matter of time before she got caught up. I wasn't trying to be involved in that mess."

Ramello nodded in understanding. "Makes sense." And he believed her.

Their connection had come as a surprise to them both, as neither of them could have anticipated what would come of their encounter. The depth. The intensity. The transparency. The love. All of it had been like nothing that they had ever experienced before. It had been a truly life-changing experience for both of them, as they brought their strengths and weaknesses together to challenge, refine, support, and uplift each other. They had transcended the kind of love that most people got to experience in the mundane world. No, it was much deeper than that. It was spiritual.

Destined.

It was the kind of connection that would be experienced only once in a lifetime.

Ramello wanted nothing more than to ensure that there would never be a time where he would have to live without her again. It was hard for him to imagine not hearing her giggles, waking up to her loving and encouraging messages, her speaking life into him when shit got rough. Living in an environment where there was a bunch of masculine energy, Dominique had been that feminine energy life-force that poured into and replenished him when he had given the world, *his* world, everything that he had.

It was her love that pushed him to be even greater than he already was. She had shown him what *genuine* love with no expectations attached was.

Dominique saw him, loved him, and loved him good. It felt so good to him, and there was no way in hell he was ever letting her go.

Once he was released from those gates, there would be no turning back for either of them. He would make sure of it.

His cell phone on his chest vibrating caught him off guard. It was Dominique calling.

He swiped the green button up, answering the call. "What you still doin' up, Miss Lady?"

"Couldn't sleep." Her voice floated through the receiver.

"Yeah, I can't either, baby. I'm glad you called me. I was thinkin' 'bout you."

"I love it when you think about me." Her voice slipped into that seductive, teasing tone that never failed to arouse him. "What was yo fine ass thinking about?"

And like always, his body reacted to her, a bulge growing in his pants. "The story of us… it's gonna be crazy when we tell our kids how we met one day."

Ramello could already see it all so clearly in his mind. He'd come home after a long day of networking and hustling to find Dominique in the kitchen in the middle of fixing his plate. Their two kids — a boy and a girl, twins — would race toward him, arms outstretched, showering him with hugs and kisses before eagerly settling at the table, waiting patiently for dinner.

He could imagine Dominique's radiant smile, her belly round and full with their third child. He'd step behind her, wrapping his long arms around her, leaning down to plant a tender kiss on her lips as his hand gently rested on her growing belly.

Dominique giggled. "Yeah, I can't wait to tell them how you were being bad and had to get sent to my office."

"And then I'ma tell 'em how I got you to start being bad with me," he teased back.

They both laughed.

He took a deep breath. "You know once we cross that line… there is no going back, right?"

She said nothing…

"There is no leaving me, Dominique." He made his point crystal clear.

"I know." Her voice was soft, choosing not to give him resistance — not that she wanted to.

"You leavin' me would be like takin' something from me, and ain't nobody ever took shit from me." The thought of her leaving him disturbed Ramello so much that he couldn't reel himself in.

She needed to know how serious he was about what he was saying.

Fucking with Ramello was like signing a contract with Death Row. There was only one way out. He'd really hate for her to try him like that.

"I feel you, baby. I really do. And I absolutely understand what you're expressing to me right now." Dominique did her best to soothe him. She didn't like the direction that his mind was going, but she understood because she had been there herself.

Conjuring up the worst-case scenario.

"I hope you do," Ramello warned for the last time.

Dominique smiled. "Mhm, you done threatening me now, bae?"

"Shit, that wasn't no threat, shawty. It's a mufuckin' promise."

"I'm sure it is... At this point, I think you just wanna hurt me." Her voice changed again, expertly turning a tense conversation into an erotic one.

"Just a little bit." Ramello altered his tone to match hers.

"Mhm. I know you wanna choke me… spank me… and punish me when I'm bad and not listening." Sucking her bottom lip between her teeth, she let out a soft moan. "There are consequences to everything, baby. I'm very much aware of that."

"I like that perspective."

"Of course you do. I do want you to keep this in mind though…"

"And what's that?" Ramello asked.

"I don't ever stay where I'm being hurt. I'm okay with dealing with whatever consequences that come as a result of my actions… and like I said, there are consequences to everything. Don't ever forget that," Dominique explained.

It only took Ramello a few seconds to piece together the message she was trying to convey in her explanation.

She'd picked up what he was putting down and had given him a warning of her own. It wasn't as direct as his promise had been, but she had done right by taking that round-about way of expressing herself. He wouldn't have taken it well had she matched his energy.

It was in these moments where she showed how much she respected him. Most people didn't take kindly to threats, but Dominique knew who she was dealing with and exactly what she was getting herself into, so she didn't take offense or become fearful. In fact, she expected nothing less. This was the same man who had a nigga knocked off to keep her and their relationship safe.

She knew *exactly* how far Ramello would go when it came to her. It was *he* that didn't know how far she would go to make her own point.

He changed the subject.

"I love you, Domonique." His tone shifted again. This time, it was calm, in a way that displayed affection and showed his defenses were down. He was sweet on her, and in moments like the one that they were having, it showed.

"And I love you more, Ramello," she responded in a playful, flirty tone.

That was the nature of their relationship. All within one conversation, it could start as something light and flirty, then quickly get intense, hot and heavy, then go right back to being light.

It was chaotic at times, but it worked for them. The last thing that they could say was that their relationship was boring. If anything, it reminded both of them what it meant to truly *feel* for another person. What they felt for each other was deeper than they could understand.

"I guess you called 'cause you just wanted to hear a nigga's voice, huh?" he asked cockily.

"Ya damn skippy," she affirmed without hesitation. He could hear the smugness in her voice.

He smiled to himself. Dominique always made her desire for him clear. In an age where women prided themselves on being independent, she had no issue walking around knowing that she was a walking reflection of him. It didn't take her long to embrace and embody the fact that she was *his*.

That made him love her all the more.

"You crazy, girl." He chuckled.

"And you love it." Dominique yawned. "I'ma let you go though. I *did* just want to hear your voice, baby. I need to get to sleep, so I can get up and come get you."

"Yeah, get some sleep, baby. I need you here RICH'S-AP!!" he emphasized.

"You know it. Goodnight."

"Gimme them lips before you go."

They kissed each other through the phone at the same time.

"Night-night, my love." Ramello ended the call.

I'm really 'bout to be up out this bitch, he thought.

The following day would mark a new beginning for Ramello. A fresh start. He had fucked up his life before, so much so that he lost seven years to the system. This would be the last time it ever kept him caged away again.

The way that he saw it, he would either die peacefully in his bed or go out in a blaze of glory. There was no in between.

CHAPTER THREE

"Aɪɢʜᴛ, Dixon, don't let me see you back in here, you hear me?" said Mrs. B, one of the corrections officers he'd gotten to know during his time inside. She buzzed him through the gate, setting him free from the prison.

"Shiiid, you won't," was all he had to offer her.

Ramello swaggered out from behind the gates, a newfound lightness in his step that hadn't been there days before. He was free, and it showed. As he reached the sidewalk, his eyes scanned the row of cars lined up outside, his heart skipping a beat when he spotted the sleek Range Rover he knew by heart. A grin stretched wide across his face the instant he saw Dominique step out, her excitement undeniable as she started running toward him.

She was stunning in a white romper that hugged her curvy figure, accentuating her thick thighs and soft curves. Her radiant skin glowed in the sunlight, while her silk-pressed hair bounced with every hurried step she took. Dominique's energy was contagious, her joy spilling out in the form of bubbly squeals as she closed the distance between them.

"Ahhh! You're really here!" she screamed, her voice high-pitched with excitement.

The moment Ramello stepped off the curb and onto the pavement beyond the prison gates, Dominique sprang forward and threw herself into his arms. He caught her effortlessly, his hands settling on her thick hips as she wrapped her arms around his neck. Her warmth enveloped him, and her familiar scent hit him like a wave — sweet, subtle, and grounding. He walked her across the street in his embrace, their lips meeting in a heated kiss that seemed to sweep away the months they'd spent apart.

Ramello positioned her back against the Range Rover's driver-side door, and Dominique cupped his face in her soft hands, her nails a perfect pop of color against his smooth chocolate skin.

"They really freed you," she said breathlessly, her eyes locked with his as he leaned his forehead against hers.

Ramello let out a shaky laugh. It almost felt surreal.

"Yeah… finally."

She could see the overwhelm of emotion in his eyes, and she leaned forward and kissed him again while still cupping his face. This kiss was gentler. Comforting. Then she hugged him again, tightening her arms around him.

Ramello buried his face in her neck, inhaled deeply, and squeezed her back, grateful for her grounding him back in his body and out of his emotion. They would have time for that later. For now, he needed to get as far away from the prison as possible.

"You smell so fuckin' good," he mumbled into her neck.

"Thank you." He felt her lips brushing against his neck in a gentle kiss.

Ramello pulled back. "Aight, I'll drive."

"Drive!?" Her tone was reminiscent of Soulja Boy on his *Breakfast Club* interview when he was asked about Drake.

Ramello laughed, walked her around to the passenger side, and opened the door for her. "Yes, baby, drive."

"Don't get to tearin' my shit up now," Dominique teased nervously.

"Man, shawty, chill. I got this." He chuckled at her skepticism. "It's like riding a bike," he added, closing the door before she could answer.

No the hell it ain't! Dominique thought to herself as she watched Ramello round the front of the car and get into the driver's seat.

"You sure you got it? It's been a while." Dominique watched as he adjusted the seat to accommodate his long legs, leaned it back to an unnecessarily low angle, and fiddled with her rearview mirrors.

"Where the ignition at?" He ignored her question.

Dominique pointed at a button on the side of the steering wheel. "It's a push start, baby."

He pushed the button, and a series of beeps sounded, and the radio came on.

Dominique giggled. She knew that there was going to be a learning curve that he would have to work through. It was one of the main pitfalls of long-term incarceration. That was something that she was prepared to walk through with him. Ramello was a quick learner, so she was confident that he would be able to work through them with ease.

"Pushing it once, you put it into accessory mode. It turns on the radio, lights, charging ports, stuff like that, and you can roll the windows up and down. To start the engine, you have to put your foot on the brake and then press the button," she explained.

Ramello followed her instructions, and the car hummed to life. He looked at her, nodding, a confident smirk on his face. "There we go!"

Dominique laughed at his expression, grabbed her phone, and put her address into the navigation system for him. "Okay, now… take it easy, sir."

"Yo man got this, girl. You just sit back and relax, baby." He put one hand on her bare thigh and began rubbing his fingertips back-and-forth on her soft and delicate skin.

Shifting the gear into drive, he slowly pulled away from the curb and began their hour-long journey back to Dominique's home in Macon. Fortunately, they hadn't needed to relocate Dominique after Ramello was transferred to Telfair. Previously, she had been commuting an hour to work at Valdosta, and with the transfer, her travel time shifted to an hour in the opposite direction.

After a few minutes of driving, Ramello had tested the brakes, gauging how much pressure he would need to put on the pedal to make a smooth turn and come to a complete stop. Besides that, it really *had* been like riding a bike. Once you knew how to do it, you couldn't forget.

Dominique exhaled a deep breath as she realized her anxiety had been for nothing. Relaxing into the passenger seat, she pulled out her phone and opened Spotify, scrolling to a playlist she had made specifically for him. Within moments, the smooth rhythm of T.I.'s *Let's Get Away* filled the car, blending seamlessly with the mood between them.

Reaching over, Dominique gently ran her manicured fingers over the nape of his neck, her nails offering a sooth-ing, rhythmic scratch against his skin. His focus stayed on the road, but he reached up with the hand resting on her thigh. Grasping her hand, he guided it away from his neck and laced their fingers together. Then, with a quiet tenderness, he kissed the back of her hand before placing it back on her thigh, trap-ping it securely between his hand and her leg.

The rest of the drive was wrapped in a comfortable, unspoken understanding. Dominique didn't fill the silence with words, giving him the space she knew he needed. Today wasn't just any day. It was his first day free, and she couldn't ignore the weight he carried. Though he remained quiet, his thoughts were evident in the furrow of his brow, the clench of his jaw, the measured way he held the steering wheel. She didn't pry; she didn't need to. The energy between them spoke louder than anything he could have said.

Instead, Dominique let the music speak for her. Each new song that played seemed to resonate, and she noticed he was listening. Every so often, without a word, he lifted her hand to his lips, pressing a gentle kiss against it — a small but meaningful gesture that told her more than any words. They didn't need to fill the air with conversation; they were already communicating in their shared, silent language.

As Ja Rule's *Mesmerize* began to play, Dominique turned her head toward him, catching his gaze for the first time in miles. A soft smile tugged at their lips, and without hesitation, they leaned in together. Their kiss was quiet and tender, a brief but powerful exchange reflecting everything they couldn't — and didn't need to — say.

BY THE TIME they pulled into her driveway, the playlist had looped once, and the sun was at its highest peak in the sky. Her spot was on the corner of a cul-de-sac, nestled between two other townhomes with matching brick exteriors, though hers had more character. The shutters were painted a soft, creamy beige that complemented the deep red brick, and a hanging fern swayed gently from a black iron hook on the porch. There was a plain, black mat that read *Who The Hell Invited You?* at the entrance of the door, and a pair of gold lanterns framed the dark green front door like subtle jewelry.

The small yard out front was clean, edged, and neat; someone had clearly been tending to it. A ring of white stones circled a young crepe myrtle tree in the grass, and a ceramic planter near the porch steps overflowed with lavender and rosemary. It didn't scream money, but it whispered it. Quiet confidence. Soft, feminine touches — just like Dominique.

Ramello let out a slow exhale he hadn't realized he'd been holding.

He could feel the weight of the past decade pressing against the glass, watching from the rearview mirror, but here, in this calm, curated corner of the world, it didn't feel as heavy. This place wasn't just her home; it was a safe space. A sanctuary.

"Damn," he muttered under his breath, half in awe, half in disbelief. "You really built somethin' for yourself."

Dominique gave him a small smile. "For us now," she corrected gently.

Ramello looked at her then back at the townhouse. It didn't feel real yet, but for the first time in a long time, it felt possible.

Dominique climbed out first, stretching her legs and letting the warm Georgia air hit her skin. Ramello lingered in the driver's seat for a moment, taking a deep breath as he stared at the house in front of him, a place that had been hers for years but would now have to hold both of them.

"You comin'?" she teased, swinging the door open wide enough for him to see her playful smirk.

Ramello stepped out, shut the door behind him, and followed her to the front porch. Every step away from that prison and toward this new chapter felt surreal — but the weight of her presence, her love, was anchoring him to the moment.

Quietly, Ramello stood behind Dominique and allowed her to open up the door for the both of them to enter. She stepped in first and flipped on the light switch, so they could navigate the living room.

Ramello stepped in behind her and quietly closed the door, turning the lock with a soft click. As his gaze traveled around the room, a warm smile spread across his face. The living room was a picture of celebration. Balloons, gifts, and rose petals adorned every corner, draping the furniture and floor in vibrant cheer. Above the green sofa, which was piled high with gifts she'd carefully chosen to welcome him into their new shared home, golden balloons floated in perfect alignment, spelling out "Welcome Home." The thoughtfulness of it all made his heart swell.

From clothes and hygiene to entertainment and new cell phones, she had thought of it all. Since the beginning of their relationship, Ramello had always made her life a little bit easier to manage by serving her in any way that he could, and when he couldn't personally take care of something, he had no issue with paying someone who could.

Dominique wanted to reciprocate that energy and had taken it upon herself to get all of his basics together for him. It may not have been much, but things like setting up his new cell phone service was something he appreciated. If nothing else, it would save him a bit of time since he no longer had to do it himself.

Dominique wrapped her arms gently around Ramello from behind, her warm embrace pulling him from his thoughts as she pressed softly against his back.

"Welcome home, Daddy," Dominique said softly, her hand resting gently on his stomach in a warm, affectionate touch.

Without a word, Ramello turned in her embrace, gently lifting her chin with his finger. His lips claimed hers, and effortlessly, they melted into each other. The kiss grew intense, their hands roaming freely, exploring and gripping one another as passion took over.

Dominique let out a soft moan as Ramello's thick tongue eased into her mouth. Their tongues intertwined in a slow, sensual rhythm, locked in an intimate dance. Ramello's hand gripped her waist firmly, while his other rested gently on the back of her neck, their lips meeting in a tender, seamless embrace.

"Bedroom?" Ramello mumbled against her neck, leaving a hot trail of kisses on her skin when she broke away to catch her breath.

"Babe, we gotta leave in a lil bit," Dominique whimpered. Her hands were underneath the black t-shirt he was wearing, caressing his defined abs.

"We'll get there when we get there. They can wait."

Effortlessly, he scooped her up, her legs instinctively wrapping around his waist as he carried her toward what he guessed was the bedroom. She clung to him, her lips trailing soft kisses across his face, pausing only to murmur directions to guide him there.

"Last door to the left."

Ramello followed her instructions into the bedroom, flipping on the light as he stepped inside. He broke away from her lips briefly, glancing around the room to locate the bed. Just as he lifted his foot to head toward it, she slipped from his arms and sank gracefully to her knees.

He bit his bottom lip, eyes fixed on Dominique as she glanced up at him through her lashes. Her delicate fingers worked to unbuckle his belt, easing his hard length free from the confines of his jeans.

"I fuckin' missed this," she whispered in awe. Wrapping her hand around his throbbing length, she stroked it gently, savoring every moment.

"Prove it," Ramello demanded.

He reached out, his hand sliding gently to the back of her head, guiding himself to her parted lips. As he eased forward, a deep moan of pleasure escaped him, his movement unhurried yet deliberate. The moment her throat tightened in reflex, her body tensing as she gagged, he paused, savoring the sensation.

After months of longing, the feeling of Dominique's warm, wet tongue and throat finally enveloping him was almost overwhelming. The way she licked, massaged, and caressed him as he moved against her sent waves of pleasure through him — a realization of the fantasies he'd been holding onto for so long.

Dominique pulled away from his dick to catch her breath and instead rubbed it back-and-forth across her juicy lips and kissed the head of it repeatedly. "I missed suckin' on it too."

She moaned and slapped his mushroom shaped tip against her tongue. Her eyes fluttered closed as she wrapped her lips around it again before slowly taking as much of it as she could down her throat.

Ramello let out a loud groan, pulling his shirt off in one motion. Shifting his weight, he leaned back against the door-frame, bracing himself before muttering a sharp, "Ugh — fuck!"

The sensation of being back in Dominique's mouth after such a long time apart was intoxicating. It stirred something deep within him, and he could already feel an orgasm beginning to build in his core. He tried his best to hold it back. He wasn't ready to succumb just yet. A low, drawn-out moan escaped his lips. That was a fight he wasn't going to win, *especially* once she added her soft ass hands to the mix. That had been her plan the entire time. To milk him for everything he had right out the gate so they could get moving with their day. She knew she wouldn't have been able to get away with not giving him *something*. So, she opted to take off a bit of the edge that she knew he was feeling. Doing so would allow him to get through his party with his family.

Dominique felt Ramello's length thicken and pulse under her touch, and she lifted her eyes to meet his. Keeping her lips wrapped tightly around the tip, she worked his spit-slicked dick skillfully with both hands, her motions firm and fluid. Moments later, his release spilled warmly into her mouth as she held his gaze, unbroken.

Ramello let out a deep, guttural groan, his body trembling as an intense wave of pleasure overtook him. It felt as though every ounce of tension had been wrung out of him, leaving him weak in its wake. His arms were stretched wide, gripping the doorframe for support, as he leaned forward, his breath ragged. Dominique's lips moved skillfully, taking him deeper as his legs threatened to give out beneath him.

"Mmmm," Dominique moaned and swallowed.

Ramello bit his bottom lip, shaking his head, eyes locked on his woman on her knees before him. "I missed you." He stood upright and extended his hands to help her to her feet. Once she was standing, he drew her close, resting his hands gently on her ass. Leaning down, he placed a soft kiss on her lips.

"Better?" Dominique asked, a smirk playing at her lips.

Ramello laughed. "Yeah, *much* better, baby. Thank you."

"Good. Now, let's hurry up and shower. We gotta get movin'." She bent down to untie his shoes for him.

His jeans and boxers were bunched around his ankles, his shoes still on. The two remained silent as he let Dominique help him finish undressing. Taking his hand, she guided him into the adjoining bathroom. He stood quietly, watching as she turned on the shower, adjusting the water until it was warm. Satisfied, she turned back to him and motioned for him to step in.

"I'll be back." He heard her voice faintly over the shower.

A minute later, she returned to the bathroom with an armful of men's hygiene products.

She literally thought of everything, Ramello thought in appreciation, watching her place body soap, shampoo, conditioner, and a few other things that he didn't know what to do with in the built-in shelf space underneath the shower head. There was a total of four shelves. The bottom two held all of Dominique's hygiene products, and she placed all of Ramello's things on the top two.

"I should have already put that stuff in there, but…" Her voice trailed off. She was speaking to herself out loud.

Ramello stood silently, his gaze locked onto Dominique as she stepped back, peeling away her clothes with effortless grace. His breath hitched as she revealed her naked, full-figured body. Dominique was a stunning, confident woman, her soft curves accentuated under the gentle light in the bathroom. Her rich, mahogany-toned skin glistened faintly, a testament to her natural beauty. Ramello's desire swelled instantly, his pulse quickening and his body responding the moment her voluptuous frame slipped into the shower beside him.

She gave him a knowing look, her almond-shaped eyes shimmering with a mix of timidity and playful confidence. Despite everything, it almost felt surreal to him — standing here with Dominique, the woman who had occupied his fantasies during so many lonely nights. She flashed him a soft smile, the kind that seemed to light up her beautiful, round face, and rose onto her tiptoes to place a gentle peck on his lips, the steam swirling around them. He stood still under the warm cascade of water, his toned body glistening damp, mesmerized by her presence and captivated by her authenticity.

Dominique's eyes roamed appreciatively over his form. Months of dedication to transform himself before his release showed in the sharp lines of his physique — the lean muscle, the discipline etched into his body. He was built like a man who had fought hard to reclaim his identity, and she admired it openly. Her smile deepened with pride, knowing she was sharing such an intimate moment with him.

She grabbed a clean white washcloth she'd set aside specifically for him, careful in her actions. Dominique squirted a generous amount of men's body wash onto the cloth, her movements slow and thoughtful as she lathered it. Stepping closer, she began to gently clean Ramello's broad chest, her soft hands brushing against his skin as she worked in unhurried, tender strokes. She took her time, savoring the connection, letting each touch convey her affection without words.

For the first time, the two shared the kind of intimacy neither of them had dared to dream about before. Under the stream of water, their interaction unfolded quietly — no words necessary. Dominique's plush body pressed lightly against Ramello's lean frame as they washed one another, their movements slow and deliberate, each touch carefully considered. It was a communion of touch, a silent language that spoke volumes about their feelings, desires, and unspoken promises.

This was the moment Ramello had often fantasized about during his time locked away — dreaming of Dominique's warmth, her beauty, and the depth of her love. Now, standing in her shower as the water cascaded over them, with her curvy figure close to him and her soft hands moving across his skin, that dream had finally come to life… and it was better than he could have ever imagined.

Throughout that moment, Ramello never once considered the idea of being intimate with Dominique in a sexual way. What he truly craved was a deeper connection, a form of intimacy that transcended mere words. They shared an unspoken understanding that sometimes a gentle touch could convey what words could not express. Every caress, stroke, and kiss they shared resonated deeply, forging a strong connection between them.

Twenty minutes later, after finishing their showers, Dominique emerged, wrapping a towel around her full figure. As she rotated to reach for another towel, she signaled for Ramello to step out. Her gaze instantly turned sultry the moment he emerged with drops of water trickling down his defined and toned chest and abs, revealing a powerful physique. His dick hanging long, hard, and heavy, he looked like a Black god.

Dominique carefully dried his body with a soft, fluffy white towel, her touch tender and deliberate. The moment felt surreal to Ramello, as if he was living a dream. Dominique embodied everything men often idealized in a submissive woman — a quiet strength wrapped in warmth and care. Maybe it was her background as a nurse, or perhaps it was simply her nature, but her nurturing qualities were genuine, not an act. Those were the traits Ramello cherished most about her.

He couldn't put a price on that.

Within minutes, they were back in the bedroom. Ramello sat on the bed while Dominique gently smoothed lotion over his skin. Her soft, delicate touch lulled him into a relaxed haze, his eyelids growing heavier with each stroke.

He couldn't tell whether it was from her draining him, the warmth of the shower, or the comforting energy that enveloped him as she straddled him in bed, gently massaging lotion into his chest and shoulders. All he knew was that it was making him drowsy, lulling him into a peaceful slumber.

Maybe it was a combination of it all.

"Okay, the clothes that I have for you are in there on the couch. You can go pick you something out to wear while I finish up in here," Dominique said and attempted to get up.

Ramello gripped her by the hips, making the towel she

was wearing fall into a pool around his hands. He couldn't help but to reach up and palm her soft breasts now that they were in his face.

"Thank you." He sat up and kissed her gently on the lips.

Dominique smiled and leaned her forehead against his. "Always."

With a final kiss, Ramello let her slip away and watched as she disappeared into the bathroom. Rising to his feet, he began to stroll through the modest townhouse, his eyes wandering over the carefully chosen décor. He couldn't help but smile as he looked around her space. It was so *Dominique*. From the color choices, the color-blocking, plants, it was all very reflective of her overall vibe. Feminine and nourishing. His smile grew bigger looking at all of the stuff that she had gotten him on the couch. It was clear all the thought, time, and effort she put into making his first day home one that he would remember. She wanted him to be as comfortable as he possibly could after having to spend years in one of the most uncomfortable places a human could be. The fact that she cared so much only made his feelings for her grow deeper. Dominique made it easy for him by having the clothes she bought him neatly folded and fitted together in outfits she could see him in. One fit in particular made him laugh.

I can't believe she even remembered this shit, Ramello thought, still chuckling.

He held a black t-shirt in the air and shook his head looking at it. On the shirt was a conceptual piece of art by one of his favorite graphic artists, Baby Alien Razy Ray. It was a reimagining of Baby D and Day Day from the movie *Next Friday*. Day Day stood behind Baby D in his Pinky's uniform shirt with his arms wrapped around her.

He burst out laughing again. *This girl don't forget shit.*

Dominique had both the best and worst memory. Though

a usually forgetful person, she still had the tendency to remember some of the most trivial shit. The shirt was in reference to a fleeting moment they'd had at the beginning of their relationship. He remembered sending her a picture of the exact shirt from the artist' page and cracking up about it. That was often how she showed and expressed her love.

Placing them to the side, Ramello searched for some draws in the sea of clothing that waited for him. There was everything from jerseys, graphic tees, undershirts, boxers, jeans, shorts, and anything else he could possibly need. After finding a pair of jeans and everything that he would need to dress himself for the day, he began putting on his clothes.

He was tying the shoestrings of his Jordan Retro 4s when Dominique walked into the living room. She fell into a fit of giggles when she saw Ramello's outfit choice. He grinned, glancing up at her as she opened the living room curtains, letting sunlight pour in. Her infectious laughter filled the room, and he couldn't help but laugh along with her.

"You like the shirt, huh?" she asked with a playful smile.

He stood up, walked over to her, and pulled her in close. "I love it."

"Good." She pecked his lips.

Dominique was fully dressed and looked good as hell. She wore a cream-colored, body-hugging, midi dress that kissed every curve without doing too much. The soft, ribbed fabric clung just right with long, mesh sleeves and a modest square neckline that showed a tasteful amount of cleavage. The color popped against her mahogany skin, glowing in the golden afternoon. Her waist was cinched with a thin gold belt that added just the right amount of shine, matching the small gold hoops in her ears and the dainty chain around her ankle — subtle but noticeable. Her heels were nude, strappy, and high enough to give her that confident sway when she walked, but she was still grounded. Still in control. Her silk press was refreshed, bone straight, and parted deep on the side, cascading past her shoulders like a waterfall. Edges laid. Her makeup was minimal with just some eyeliner and lashes that curled like whispers. And her scent? Warm, sweet, expensive. A layered blend of vanilla, sandalwood, and something darker that lingered just long enough to make people turn their heads after she passed. Dominique didn't need to do the most; she was the most. And today, she was showing up as Ramello's peace, his prize, and his woman. He beamed down at her with adoration.

"What?" she asked, blushing under his gaze. A nervous giggle followed.

"Nothin'… I'm just not used to seeing you outside of work clothes." He grabbed her by the dress and tugged her toward him. "You look good." He smiled and gave her a nod of approval.

"I like this too, but I don't know how yo folks gonna feel about the shirt." She laughed and tugged on the hem.

He smiled. "Shiiid, they know me."

CHAPTER FOUR

RAMELLO PULLED into the driveway of his mama's house and barely got the car in park before the front door swung open, and three kids came barreling down the steps yelling his name.

"Uncle Mello!"

He threw the door open with a grin, stepping out just in time to catch the youngest in mid-air. Her braids smacked him in the face as she clung tightly around his waist. The other two latched on — one to his legs, the other to his side — and he couldn't help but laugh, completely consumed by the joyful chaos. The unmistakable scent of barbecue smoke mingling with somebody's overpowering perfume wafted from the porch, hitting him all at once and grounding him in the moment.

He was home.

Dominique stepped out a beat after him, letting him have his moment. She stayed close but not too close. She wasn't the type to make an entrance louder than the person she came for.

The kids ran ahead to tell everybody he was really here, and that was when the porch started to fill. Aunties, cousins, old neighbors, folks he hadn't seen in years spilled out with drinks in hand and big smiles on their faces. His mama stepped out last, moving slow like she'd been holding back tears since breakfast.

Dominique's face lit up when she saw her. "Mrs. Dixon!" she called out with warmth as she moved to embrace her. "I was about to come get you myself."

His mom waved her off with a smile and hugged her tight. "Girl, I told you to stop callin' me that. It's Mama D now."

Dominique laughed. "Okay, Mama D."

"Let me look at you," Mama D said, holding her at arm's length. "You even prettier in person. Got my son out here cheesin' like the damn Kool-Aid man."

"I can't help that," Dominique said with a playful shrug.

Ramello smirked at them from the side, watching two of the most important women in his life talk like they'd been friends forever.

They kind of had.

They'd been on the phone plenty, texted even more. Mama D already knew her favorite color, what kind of wine she liked, and the name of the candle she kept burning in her kitchen. This was just the first time they were sharing air.

And it felt right.

Ramello slid his arm around Dominique's waist and looked around the yard. "I know y'all ain't waitin' on me to eat, right?"

"Yes, nigga! We *were* actually," one of his aunties chimed in from somewhere off to the side.

Laughter broke out from the crowd.

"You lucky we like you," somebody else shouted from the grill.

The vibe was exactly what it needed to be, like a family reunion but turned down just enough for folks to really catch up. Lawn chairs were in clusters, kids were chasing bubbles, and music rode the breeze low and steady. Dominique moved through it effortlessly. She kept close when needed, but mostly, she floated, helping the aunties pass out plates, holding babies on her hip, and laughing with his little cousins who'd already nicknamed her *Domo*.

Ramello watched her from a folding chair on the porch with a Pepsi in hand, posted up next to his Uncle Henry, and smiling to himself. She was in her element — soft but grounded, shining but not loud. People noticed her, not because she demanded attention but because her presence *pulled* it.

"She somethin' else," his uncle muttered, nodding in her direction.

"Yeah," Ramello said, still looking at her. "She is."

"I like the shirt." He pointed at his shirt. "She a biggin'!"

He nodded in approval and dapped Ramello up, who laughed at his assessment.

Uncle Henry leaned back in his folding chair, gold tooth catching the sunlight, the smell of his Old Spice cologne mixed with weed cutting through the barbecue smoke. He had on a fitted hat, a white button up shirt open halfway down his chest, and a gold chain with a cross that looked older than Ramello, a walking relic of the Player's Hall of Fame.

"Boy, lemme tell you somethin'. When you got a woman like that, one that look good, smell good, and make a plate for you without askin', you *hold on*. You hear me?"

Ramello laughed. "I hear you, Unc."

Henry sipped from his cup and gave a little hum. "Done got me a good one myself since you been away. Real grown." He glanced sideways, voice dipping into that confidential, playa-to-playa register. "She run shit down at Hartsfield-Jackson. Big badge. *Head* of TSA."

"You bullshittin'," Ramello said in disbelief.

Henry grinned, eyes crinkling. "I shit you not, nephew! Got her own key card and everything. She can get a pitbull on a muthafuckin' plane if she wanted to."

Ramello laughed again, shaking his head. "Man, where you be findin' these women?"

Uncle Henry adjusted his hat. "They find *me*, nephew. Old school charm still work in this new school world. Women just want a man who smell like cash and mind his bidness."

"You ain't got no money, Unc."

Henry did a double take. "Who ain't got no money!? Shiiid, that's what I want y'all to think. I don't need nobody callin' askin' me for nothin'!"

Ramello couldn't stop laughing. He could always count on his uncle to keep him in tears. "Maaan, gone 'head on, Unc."

"I'm for real. Shooot."

"Henry!" someone yelled from the yard to the left.

Ramello and Henry turned to see that it was a stocky, bald guy at the Spades table, but Ramello didn't recognize him. He assumed that he was a friend of the family.

"What, Ray?" Uncle Henry was sitting up now.

"Don't I owe you an ass whoopin' on these cards? Quit runnin' ya mouth and come get cooked."

"Never seen anybody in such a rush to take a L in my life," Henry yelled back. "Hold on, nephew. Looks like I gotta school me one."

He stood with a groan, smoothing his shirt and limping off toward the Spades table like a man with stories he'd never tell. Ramello watched him go, smiling to himself.

Old playas didn't die. They just moved smoother.

He put his attention back on Dominique, who seemed to be getting along with everybody, but of course someone was on the bullshit. His cousin, Toya, sat under a tree with her usual wine glass and even more usual side-eye. She had the kind of energy that made the air shift whenever someone she didn't like walked past. Dominique clocked it but didn't let it faze her. She just smiled, nodded, and kept it moving whenever Toya tried to force herself into her bubble.

The day went on, and Ramello had been able to get a moment by himself and took it as an opportunity to make a second plate. There was no one in the house, and he used it to take some time to decompress and process how he was feeling. He was in the midst of making his plate when his Toya walked into the kitchen.

"She pretty. I'll give her that," she said, sipping on her fourth glass of wine that evening.

Ramello didn't look at her. "But?"

"What?" She laughed. "I wasn't finna say nothin' bad."

Ramello glanced over at Toya, raising an eyebrow. "You sure? You always got somethin' to say."

She smirked, leaning on the counter. "Not this time. She cool. Real cool actually. Just surprised you brought somebody."

"Why's that?" he asked, cautiously curious.

"'Cause it's you, Melo. You don't bring folks around like that. But… I like her. Don't mess it up."

Ramello chuckled softly, shaking his head. "Appreciate it, Toya. Really."

Toya shrugged, taking another sip. "Don't get used to it. Next party, I'm back to my usual self."

"I'm countin' on it."

And with that, she walked away, leaving him to turn his attention back to the plate in front of him and the ribs sizzling on the grill that were visible through the kitchen window. A grin spread across his face. He was impressed. Dominique had done the impossible: she'd gotten Toya's approval. That simply *never* happened. Toya, the family's self-proclaimed "messy cousin", had a gift for hating everyone's company and an even greater talent for stirring up drama. It was her thing. But Dominique? She'd somehow broken through, leaving everyone — including him — stunned.

Not that it would've mattered to him either way. Dominique wasn't something to question or debate in his mind; she was solid. Still, the fact that she'd managed to pull it off was the kind of surprise he didn't see coming.

What is there not to love, I guess? he thought.

Later, as the sky shifted into a peachy gold and the music mellowed into old-school slow jams, Ramello and Dominique stood side by side, plates empty, full in other ways. She leaned into him just a little, her hand brushing his without grabbing it, and he bumped her softly with his shoulder.

"You alright?" she asked with a knowing look.

"I'm better than alright," he said, his eyes on her. "You?"

"I'm good. Your folks coo."

"Most of 'em," he said with a grin. "They good though."

She smirked, not asking for details. She already knew.

As the sun began to set, they finally made their exit, exchanging goodbyes and waving from the car as it pulled away.

Dominique gripped the steering wheel, focused, while Ramello lounged in the passenger seat, his chair tilted back as he rested, recharging. The atmosphere between them buzzed with a quiet intensity — electric yet peaceful, as if everything was steadily falling into place.

Ramello couldn't stop staring at her as she drove them to their next destination.

"You worked that room," he said, voice low, eyes intently watching her.

"I know," Dominique said and flipped her hair smugly. "I had to give you sum' to brag about."

He smirked and reached over to squeeze her thigh. "And that you did, baby. That you did."

HOURS LATER, they arrived in Savannah, just past Tybee Island. The sky was a deep indigo, draped like velvet over the horizon as they pulled up to a quiet dock. A gentle breeze stirred the water, carrying the mingling scents of salt and something sweet. Dominique stepped out first, her heels clicking softly against the wooden planks, followed closely by Ramello. Ahead of them, the yacht stood tall and graceful against the night — its sleek white frame bathed in a warm amber glow, casting a soft, candlelight-like shimmer over the dark, rippling water.

"Damn," Ramello muttered low under his breath. "A nigga ain't expect all this..."

Dominique smiled, a coy glint in her eyes. "You deserve it."

The captain greeted them briefly before disappearing into the lower deck, leaving them to explore the space alone. The yacht was private and intimate. Meant for two. A table had already been set on the top deck under a canopy of twinkling fairy lights. Champagne on ice. A low playlist of slow, sultry R&B wrapped around them like velvet. There wasn't a full meal waiting. That had already been taken care of hours ago at his momma's. This was about indulgence. Decadence. Pleasure.

Dessert.

Two chairs faced each other at the small table, but Ramello chose to stand behind Dominique and pull hers out for her like a gentleman. She sat with a quiet smile, legs crossed, her dress hiking up, exposing her thick thighs.

Ramello sat across from her, his eyes never leaving her face. He'd seen her laughing with his aunties earlier, scooping mac and cheese on kids' plates, dapping up his uncle. And now, here she was, glowing under moonlight and music. A different kind of magic.

"Alright," Dominique said, lifting the silver lid from the platter at the center of the table. "Dessert's served."

Inside, chocolate-dipped strawberries, thick slices of still warm peach cobbler, two scoops of vanilla bean ice cream already starting to melt, and glossy squares of milk chocolate stacked beside miniature glasses of amber-colored cognac rested on the platter.

Ramello leaned back in his chair, lips parted, eyes scanning the tray before returning to her.

"You tryna seduce me?"

Dominique smirked, savoring the moment as she lifted a strawberry to her lips and bit into it with deliberate ease. "I'm tryna spoil you."

"Same thing."

She slid the tray a little closer then dipped a second strawberry in the pool of chocolate and held it out for him. He leaned in, biting it from her fingers, slow and deliberate, letting the juice spill onto his tongue before licking the tip of her finger clean. Her breath hitched just a little.

They fed each other like that, strawberries, bites of cobbler, sips of the dark liquor that warmed the back of their throats. Ramello wasn't much of a drinker, but he decided that he would indulge with his woman that night.

Dominique broke off pieces of chocolate and pressed them to his lips. Ramello trailed his fingers down her arm as she sipped from her glass, watching the way her throat moved as she swallowed. Everything about her was soft and inviting — like she was made for him.

The dessert course melted into something slower, a shared heat between them, growing with every exchanged glance and graze of their fingers.

Once they had finished their dessert, Ramello grabbed

Dominique by the hand from across the table and tugged on her fingers for her to stand and come sit in his lap. Without him having to utter a word, she gracefully stood and lowered her ass into his lap.

"I just wanted to make sure that I took the time to tell you that I appreciate all the effort that you put into making today a good day for me, Dominique. You really made today a lot easier with making sure that I had the things that I would need, and I didn't even have to bathe myself.

"And seeing you with my family and the way that you just blended the fuck in means more to me than you'll probably ever know. I am in love with you, Dominique. I didn't see you coming, but I'm hella grateful that I found you, baby." Ramello poured his heart out.

Tears welled in Dominique's eyes as she listened to his confession of love. She was glad that her sentiments were reciprocated.

"And I'm in love with you too, Ramello. I didn't see you comin' either, but I know it's no coincidence that we crossed paths. Since I've met you, you've been nothing but good to me. You make me better. You make me wanna do better. Be better. Strive for greater. You came into my life and showed me how to love and *feel* again.

"When I had no one, you were there. When it was hard for me to love myself, you were there. Loving me through it all. When I'm down, you never fail to pour into me. You've done more for me behind a prison wall than anyone in my life who was free. It's easy for me to love you because every day you make me feel how much you love me. All I want is to give you that back in return, Melly baby." Dominique stared deeply into Ramello's eyes, her fingertips caressing his cheeks.

Ramello's throat was thick with emotion as he listened to

her express her love for him. She had left him speechless, unsure of what to say next.

He didn't need to say a word. Dominique stood up from his lap, extending her hand toward him. Ramello didn't have to ask where they were headed.

She led him below deck, down the narrow staircase, into the cozy cabin lit with dim amber light. A bed — wide, plush, and dressed in ivory linen — sat against the back wall. Floor-to-ceiling windows surrounded it, offering a view of the water and the cityscape reflecting in it.

It felt like a floating dream.

Ramello stepped closer behind her, wrapping his arms around her waist. His hands slid up, fingers tracing her collarbone, pulling her back against him. He kissed her shoulder slowly, taking his time like he didn't want to waste a second.

"You keep doin' shit like this," he murmured against her skin, "I'ma put a baby in you *RICH'SAP!*"

Dominique leaned her head back on his shoulder and giggled. "Here you go…"

He turned her around to face him and kissed her deeply, gripping her by the front of her dress.

She gently pushed him away, her eyes wild with lust. "I'm gonna go change, and when I get back… I want you in that bed, naked. Okay?"

Ramello leaned in for one last kiss before playfully giving her a light slap on the ass. As she headed to the bathroom, he watched her for a moment before turning his attention to her request. Without hesitation, he stripped off his clothes and slipped into bed, ready and waiting.

He laid back against the pillows, legs spread slightly, one arm tucked behind his head as the other rested across his stomach. Naked, warm, and full off strawberries, cobbler, and cognac, he waited, eyes fixed on the doorway like a man expecting a miracle.

And that was exactly what walked in.

Dominique descended the narrow steps with purpose, each movement slow and deliberate, like she was savoring the moment. The soft click of her heels against the hardwood drew his eyes downward, catching the glimmer of her anklet, before his gaze traveled up… and kept rising.

She was breathtaking. The deep wine-colored lingerie hugged her curves like it was made for her — rich and sultry, and the fabric gleamed like crushed velvet under the cabin's warm amber light. The 38DD bra framed her full, rounded breasts perfectly, sheer enough to hint at what lay beneath while leaving much to savor. Strappy details accented her voluptuous figure with little gold touches that caught the light — one shimmering charm nestled between the cups, another tracing the curve of her lush full hips where the garter belt cinched her waist. Her panties were high cut, sculpted to flatter her soft juicy thighs, the lace teasing the dip of her hips and the fullness of her ass in a way that made Ramello's chest tighten.

Her stockings stretched taut over her shapely legs, sheer and smooth, connecting to delicate gold clasps that gleamed faintly as she moved. The little details — the glittering anklet, the elegant sway of her lingerie — all drew attention to her, as if she carried a quiet power in her every step.

Her bone-straight hair fell in an ebony cascade over her shoulders, parting deep to frame her round, gorgeous face. Her makeup was flawless — long lashes framing her low, smoldering gaze, full lips glossed and slightly parted, like an unspoken invitation that sent electricity crackling through the air. Ramello felt his breath catch, as if he were witnessing something divine.

The music from upstairs grew louder so that they could hear it pulsing from above. Ramello recognized the melody to be Beyoncé's *Dance For You.*

And as if on cue… she began to move.

No words. No need.

Just the slow sway of her hips as she walked toward the bed. She didn't rush. She danced in a way that wasn't choreographed. Instead, it was feminine instinct, raw seduction with a soft smile playing on her lips. Her hands grazed her own thighs as she turned, letting him get a full view of her ass from behind. She rolled her hips to the beat that pulsed above deck then bent low, teasing the straps of her garter with her fingertips before rising again, back arched, chest lifted.

Ramello's mouth went dry.

She straddled him without touching him at first, hovering just above his lap. Her eyes met his, slow and seductive. She placed her hands on his chest, dragging her nails down his torso as her hips began to roll, soft, teasing, like she was dancing on the edge of something neither of them could escape.

"You like?" she whispered, voice low and warm.

Ramello's hands found her waist like magnets. "You already know I do."

She leaned in close, her lips ghosting across his jaw then his ear.

"Good," she purred. "Because I wore this just for you to take it off."

And that was exactly what he did.

Slow and purposeful, Dominique let him unwrap her like a gift he'd waited years to receive.

"You're so fuckin' beautiful, Dominique," Ramello mumbled in awe as he hovered over her.

He was laying between her thighs, his warm flesh pressed firmly against hers. He could feel the heat radiating from her pussy, making his desire to fill her flare up even more, but he resisted.

Time was something that hadn't been their friend when

they were having sex inside the prison. But right then and there, they had all of the time that they could possibly need.

That was the best part about that night. No longer did Ramello have to *yearn* and *long* to be with and inside of her. There was nothing confining him anymore. Now he could indulge in her as much as he wanted to.

"Mmm," Dominique moaned when he buried his face in the crook of her neck and began suckling on the tender flesh just below her earlobe. "Thank you, baby."

Ramello took his time kissing and licking nearly every exposed piece of flesh on her body. Her breath hitched the lower his mouth got on her body. She let out a soft moan when he dipped his tongue into her belly button.

She gasped when Ramello suddenly pushed her thighs back and spread her wide, so he could *really* get a taste of the dessert that he was craving.

"Oh, Ramello, baby…" Dominique's eyes rolled into the back of her head the moment she felt his tongue snaking through the slick folds of her wet pussy. "I missed feeling those lips on my pussy."

His name falling off her lips was like music to his ears, and he let out a moan of his own in acknowledgement of her words. He was too busy eating to talk.

Ramello used the tip of his tongue to circle her engorged clit then wrapped his lips around it and sucked gently. Then, he began to lap at it gently until her thighs began quaking from so much pleasure.

"Mhmm, cum for me, baby." He removed his lips from her pussy long enough to mumble to her. Then, he added his middle finger to the mix, curling it against her g-spot at the same time he sucked on her clit.

"Fuck, fuck, fuck! I'm cu…" She erupted before she could get all of the words out.

Ramello slurped her dry and used his thumb to rub and apply pressure to her asshole as she came hard all over his face and lips. He had to lay one long arm across both of her thighs to keep them from closing in around his head. He wasn't done and had every intention on pushing her to her limits.

He had waited a long time for this very day. He wanted it to last as long as it possibly could. If that meant he was going to have to give her multiple orgasms, then he was going to do exactly that.

"Okay, wait, wait, ah — wait!" Dominique was doing her best to try to get away from Ramello's tongue. He had made her cum and didn't stop eating. Her clit was overstimulated, and the pleasure was almost too much for her to bear.

There was no amount of wiggling and squirming that was going to be able to free her from his grasp.

Ramello tapped her thigh lightly, pulling his face from between her thighs. "How I'ma take care of her if you keep movin', Mama?" He kissed her pussy softly. "Huh? How I'ma take care of this pussy?" He gave her swollen lips a firm slap. "Stay still for Daddy." Sucking her clit into his mouth, he continued his tongue assault.

The rest of the night was slow, sensual. No rush. Just the rhythm of water rocking gently under them, the faint sound of the music still drifting from above, and the warmth of two bodies rediscovering each other without pressure and noise.

Just breath.

Skin.

Connection.

And when they finally curled into one another under the soft linen sheets, the moonlight spilling in over their bodies, Ramello stared at the ceiling with her tucked against his chest.

He didn't know what tomorrow held. But in that moment, surrounded by still water, silk sheets, and strawberry-sweet kisses…

He knew he was exactly where he was supposed to be.

CHAPTER FIVE

DOMINIQUE STIRRED as the early light filtered through the sheer curtains of the yacht's cabin, casting golden streaks across the plush bedding. The boat rocked gently beneath them, cradling her into a slow awakening. Her body was sore in the best ways, still humming with the afterglow of the amazing first night home that she had with Ramello.

She turned her head on the pillow and smiled.

Ramello laid beside her naked, fast asleep, with one arm slung around her waist, sprawled out like a king without a crown. The light from the sun bounced off his dark skin. Those lips that she loved kissing so much were slightly parted, full enough to recall every place they'd been on her.

His waves were a little flattened on one side from sleep but still sharp and neat, evidence of a man who took care of himself, even when life didn't always return the favor. His thick nose, strong jaw, and ruggedly handsome face was softened in his rest. And those dark brown eyes, usually so alert and calculating, were hidden behind heavy lids, his lashes kissing the tops of his cheeks.

Peace looks good on him, she thought, taking in every detail of his handsome face. The way his chest rose and fell in slow, steady breaths grounded her into reality. He looked younger in his rest, like the weight he carried had finally taken a break. She prayed that he would be able to keep it off of him.

Eventually, his lashes fluttered open, and their eyes met.

"Mornin'," she whispered with a smile, her voice still raspy from sleep.

"Mmm." He pulled her closer, kissing her shoulder. "Wanna spend the day outside. Sun feel good today."

He turned his face toward the sun shining through the windows. It felt amazing. He had spent years being inside. He was ready to be outside and have some fun.

She stretched. "I'm down. What you thinkin'? Picnic? Walk on the riverwalk? Kayaks?"

Ramello chuckled, voice still gravelly. "Nah… one of my partnas told me we should slide when we was at my mama house yesterday. There's a day party. Pool, drinks, music, ass everywhere. Real hoodrat shit. You wit' it?"

"Hell yeah! Why didn't you just say so in the first place?" Dominique giggled. "We gotta stop and get me a new bathing suit first though!"

THE SUN WAS ALREADY BLESSING the pavement when Dominique and Ramello stepped out for the day. Georgia heat kissed every inch of skin not covered by fabric, and the energy in the air buzzed with weekend promise. After leaving the yacht, they had returned home to shower and get dressed. From McCrae to Macon, to Atlanta to Savannah, back to Macon, then to Atlanta again, it felt like they were on a tour of Georgia. Ramello leaned against the car, shirtless, his chest glistening in the sun, while Dominique locked the front door.

She wore one of his oversized white tees with nothing but

black boy shorts underneath, legs bare and moisturized, toes freshly done.

"You look too good to be out here like that." He smirked, watching her with that hungry look that always made her thighs clench.

"I'm with you, ain't I?" she tossed back with a wink, brushing past him to get in the car.

An hour and a half later, Dominique finally stepped out of the dressing room wearing a sleek black two-piece. The sight was so stunning that Ramello couldn't help but stare, frozen in place, until she snapped her fingers twice to break his trance. "Don't get us kicked out this store, boy."

"Shit, they lucky I don't fuck you in the mirror right now."

After some playful back-and-forth and a few outfit swaps, she settled on a bold, tropical-print bikini with sheer mesh pants and a matching scarf tied around her hair like a hood goddess. Ramello chose some shorts, slides, and a white tank to match her vibe. Gold chains gleaming, they were *outside.*

BY THE TIME they pulled up to the party, the beat of bass was vibrating through the block. The backyard was full of half-naked bodies, grill smoke, liquor flowing, and the kind of organized chaos that only hood day parties could serve. Red Solo cups littered the ground, a kiddie pool had already been turned into a wrestling ring for drunk homegirls, and an inflatable bounce house sagged under the weight of grown ass men.

It was exactly the kind of energy Dominique didn't know she needed.

Ramello kept her hand in his as they entered, his presence shielding but never suffocating. He introduced her to a few of his boys but let her roam and shine. Dominique lit up like summer personified, laughing with girls she didn't know and dancing barefoot on the grass, her curls wild and her smile wilder. She flirted shamelessly, smacked asses, and made out with a caramel-skinned girl by the pool, while Ramello posted up with his friends, catching up on what he had missed while he was gone. He never took his eyes off his woman and the show she was putting on for him. For *everyone*.

His girl was a fuckin' vibe. A walking fantasy. And what made him proud wasn't how she looked but how damn free she was. That shit turned him on more than anything.

"Yo girl out here makin' bitches question they sexuality," one of his homeboys joked, nodding toward the pool where Dominique had slid between two girls and started spraying them both with a water gun.

"Shiiid, I would question it too if I was a bitch," another one of his partnas chimed in and dapped Ramello up.

"Where you find her?" another asked. "I know she got some fine ass friends."

"Pft." Ramello waved him off. "You don't…"

Right as he was about to respond, he saw her.

Sierra.

He just so happened to be glancing to where the backyard gate was and saw her stepping onto the scene, looking like trouble in Fashion Nova, faux butterfly locs, and a pair of platform sandals. She was hanging off one of the young niggas, but her eyes weren't on him. They were on Dominique. Watching her. *Glued* to her. Not like a friend. Not even like an enemy.

But like a woman scorned.

Ramello's jaw flexed. He didn't move right away but instead just observed. Dominique was in the pool, head tilted back in laughter, while one of the girls between her legs kissed on her thighs underwater. Sierra looked livid watching it all go down.

Nah. This shit ain't een goin' down like that, Ramello thought. Without a word, he stood to his feet and made his way through the crowd, keeping a cool stride until he was next to Sierra.

"You good?" he asked, low and blunt.

Sierra didn't look at him. "She really out here lettin' hoes eat her pussy at a party?"

Ramello smiled, but it didn't reach his eyes. "She can do whatever the fuck she want. She grown. I ain't gotta keep her on a leash for her to respect me."

Sierra finally looked at him. "You really think she solid like that?"

Ramello stepped closer, voice low and heavy. "I think you need to figure out what exactly your interest is in her before I start thinking it's a threat."

Sierra blinked.

"You gon' be a problem?" he asked flatly. "*Again?*"

She didn't answer.

He didn't need her to.

As Dominique floated on her back in the pool, laughter erupting from the women beside her, something made her pause — that sensation of being watched, too heavy, too personal. She glanced around the yard, but everything looked normal. Still, the unease lingered like the shadow of a memory she couldn't place.

HALF AN HOUR LATER, Dominique excused herself to the house to use the bathroom. She stepped into the dimly lit bathroom, the sound of the party still ringing through the walls as she quickly fixed her hair in the mirror. She walked out and there Sierra was, standing by the door, arms crossed, her usual confident stance replaced by something more subdued. The last few days had been a tense quiet between them, a distance that neither of them had bridged yet.

Sierra glanced up at her, her eyes a little more tired than usual, her usual fire replaced with a flicker of uncertainty. She cleared her throat, the silence stretching between them like an unspoken weight.

"I owe you an apology," Sierra started, her voice quieter than Dominique was used to hearing. "For what I said the last time we talked... about you being brainwashed and all that... I didn't mean it."

Dominique didn't respond immediately. Her body stiffened, a knot forming in her stomach. Sierra had been avoiding her, her words lingering in the air after the argument that felt like it had broken something. Now, seeing her standing there, looking almost... vulnerable, it stirred something in Dominique.

Sierra sighed, running a hand through her locs. "I've been thinking about it, you know. I was just hurt, and I took it out on you. I miss you, Dom. I miss *us*."

Dominique's heart skipped. This was a conversation she wasn't ready to have, but there was no sense in running from it. The tension that had been brewing in the air was too thick to ignore. Her eyes narrowed slightly as she crossed her arms over her chest, her mood shifting the moment she started remembering what was said and done.

"You don't get to talk to me like that and then act like nothing happened." Dominique's voice was steady but firm. "You've been holding on to some resentment, and I can't pretend like it doesn't bother me."

Sierra looked at her, guilt flashing across her face. "I know. And I've been trying to work through it. It's just... this situation with Ramello, it's a lot to take in. And I–I don't like the way he's got you. You're different now. But I see how happy he makes you, and I can't hate that. I don't want to."

Dominique's heart clenched. She had heard what Sierra had said, but it still didn't sit right with her.

"Sierra, I don't have the energy to keep walking on eggshells around you. I'm not going to stand by and let you call me all kinds of shit and act like you the only one hurt in this situation. I'm hurt too."

A dark skin guy with mohawk-dreads walked pass them with two big super soaker water guns, headed back to the pool.

Sierra opened her mouth to respond, but Dominique cut her off. "Listen, I'm not asking you to love Ramello. I'm not even asking you to like him. But if you can't get your shit together, if you can't stop resenting me for living my life how I want, then we can't be friends anymore. I won't allow it. Not like this."

The weight of Dominique's words hung in the air, and for a moment, neither of them spoke. Sierra's face softened, and Dominique could see the quiet struggle in her eyes.

"I get it," Sierra whispered. "I'll try, Dom. I promise I'll try. I don't want to lose you. Not over this."

Dominique's gaze softened, but she stood her ground. "You better. I can't keep putting my energy into someone who's not trying to do the same."

Just as she was about to step away, Sierra reached out and grabbed her wrist. "I'll make it right. I swear."

Dominique nodded, pulling herself from Sierra's grasp. "I hope so."

As she walked out of the house, the party noise outside seemed louder than ever. She couldn't shake the feeling that things were about to shift again between her and Sierra, but at least there was some glimmer of hope.

The heat of the backyard was crazy, and the bass-heavy

music hit her chest like a second heartbeat. Her curls were damp at the edges from pool water and sweat, her skin glowing under the Georgia sun. She didn't see Ramello at first and scanned the crowd until she spotted him leaning against the patio railing, a half-empty cup in hand.

He was watching her.

The moment their eyes locked, his relaxed posture straightened just slightly. Something in her face had changed. It wasn't her smile. She was still beautiful, still poised, but her spirit had shifted. There was a subtle tightness in the corners of her mouth, a silent weight behind her eyes.

She crossed the yard toward him, towel slung over one shoulder, and when she reached him, he offered the cup wordlessly. She shook her head.

"You good?" he asked, keeping his tone light, but his eyes studied her closely.

Dominique hesitated. It wasn't long but long enough for him to notice.

"Yeah." She sighed. "We talked. She knows where I stand now."

Ramello's jaw tensed slightly as he set his drink on the railing behind him. "And?" he asked, eyes narrowed.

Dominique ran her fingers through her curls and looked out at the crowd. "And... we'll see if she keeps her word. But if she doesn't, she knows what's up."

Ramello watched her for a beat longer. She was trying to keep it cool, trying to stay above it, but he knew her, knew when her shoulders were carrying more than they should.

"She say some slick shit to you?" he asked.

Dominique didn't answer right away. That was enough of an answer.

Ramello stepped closer. "You don't have to do that. Stop carrying her feelings and making room for her drama. She ain't earned that from you."

Dominique was quiet, looking up at him. "I just… I don't want to go back to how things were. But I'm not about to keep begging her to respect me either."

He nodded, jaw tight now.

They stood together in silence for a few seconds. Then, Ramello's gaze shifted past her and into the crowd again. He spotted Sierra near the fence line, sipping from a cup, her attention trained on them like she was trying to hear through glass.

Watching again. Always watching.

The look in her eyes wasn't curiosity. It was hunger.

Ramello tilted his head, his entire body language shifting into something colder.

Dominique noticed. "What are you thinking?"

He didn't answer at first, just handed her the towel from her shoulder and kissed her cheek.

"Lemme talk to her real quick," he said against her skin, voice low and steady like a loaded gun.

Dominique's stomach fluttered, not from nerves but from the chill in his tone. She knew that look.

"You sure?" she asked.

He stepped back, already on the move.

"Yeah," he said. "You handled yours. Now I'ma handle mine."

As Ramello moved toward Sierra, Dominique stayed behind, watching the scene unfold. She had drawn her line. Now, it was time to see if Sierra would step over it.

He moved with purpose through the crowd, his tall frame cutting through the noise and sweat and smoke of the day party until he was standing beside her.

Sierra looked up at him without flinching. Her lips curled into something that wasn't quite a smile. He had already spoken to her, so she didn't understand why he was trying it again. She resisted the urge to roll her eyes.

"What's good, Ramello?" she asked casually, like she hadn't been staring a hole through his woman.

"You tell me," he said, not bothering with small talk. "You makin' my woman uncomfortable with all your staring."

Sierra scoffed, looking away briefly before meeting his eyes again. "Ain't nothin' wrong with watchin'. Look at her, that's not the Mini I know. I just think she different now. You changed her."

Ramello stepped closer, towering over her slightly. "Change and growth are two different things, but I don't expect you to know the difference. I ain't changed her. She's just more herself now, and you can't stand that she don't need to shrink to make space for you anymore."

He could see right through her and her bullshit.

Sierra's jaw tightened, but she didn't say anything.

"She told me about y'all's history," Ramello continued, his voice low but sharp. "Whatever y'all shared... that intimacy, that closeness, those lil' unspoken moments? That shit's over wit'. Dead. She might have room in her heart for you, but I got her soul now. And I'll step on anything that threatens that."

He let the words settle. Sierra blinked slowly, chewing on the inside of her cheek.

"She ain't yours, and she ain't ever been yours," he added. "You'll never have her the way *I* have her."

Sierra's lip twitched, but she held it down.

"I see the way you look at her. Like you tryna remember what she tastes like. Like you mad she ain't yours to claim."

She looked away, her silence saying everything he needed to hear.

Ramello leaned in just enough so she could hear him over the music, his tone dark and deliberate.

"So, let me ask you *again*, Sierra. You gon' be a problem?"

She didn't answer. Didn't have to.

He tilted his head slightly, letting his next words cut with the quiet edge of a warning.

"'Cause if you are… I'll handle you. You know I will."

The space between them buzzed with unspoken heat, not sexual but dangerous.

Ramello didn't wait for a reply. He stared her down for a second longer then turned his back on her like she was nothing more than an afterthought.

Because to him, she *was*.

Dominique was across the yard now, drying off with a towel after getting out of the pool for the umpteenth time, catching her breath and laughing with a woman over a shared shot. Ramello made his way back toward her without looking back.

Sierra stayed rooted in place, face hot, pride bruised.

Her throat felt tight. She hated that her chest ached watching them together. Hated that she had to fight the heat crawling up her neck. She wasn't supposed to care this much. Wasn't supposed to feel this *replaced*.

CHAPTER SIX

THE DOOR CLICKED behind them as they stepped into the townhouse, the heavy thud sealing out the wild chaos of the day. Dominique kicked off her shoes by the entryway, her purse dropping carelessly to the floor as she slipped out of her cover-up, leaving only the tiny black bikini that had held her all day. Her skin still glistened from the heat and the pool, the faint scent of coconut sunscreen clinging to her.

She collapsed back onto the couch with a sigh. "God-damn," she muttered, eyes half-lidded. "My soul still somewhere back at that party."

Ramello laughed softly, locking the door behind them and tossing their keys on the table. He peeled off his crisp white tee, revealing the smooth, lean lines of his chest, still warm from the sun. His black shorts hung low, and the faint outline of his waves glistened with a touch of sweat.

"That party was a whole damn movie," he said, settling beside her, legs spread, confident and easy. "You see ol' girl fall off that roof into the pool?"

"She broke the chair and her dignity." Dominique snorted, a low laugh rolling out. "I needed all that today. Every second of it."

He traced lazy circles on her hip with his thumb. "You was lit, bae. I ain't never seen you that free before."

She turned her head just enough to catch his gaze, eyelashes fluttering against her cheeks. "I ain't never felt that free before. Not like that."

Their eyes locked, the air thickening between them with unspoken desire. No need for words, the slow burn always came alive when everything got quiet.

Ramello's hand found her bare thigh, fingers sliding up under the bikini bottom, cool skin heating under his touch.

"I'm tired," Dominique whispered, voice low and husky.

He smirked, pulling her up and into his arms. "C'mon then. Let me show you how to really wind down."

They moved toward the bedroom, the warm light casting soft shadows on their skin. The moment the door clicked shut, Dominique pressed against him, lips tracing his neck, teeth grazing just enough to make him groan.

Her hands explored the ridges of his back as he sank onto the bed, pulling her down with him. The silk of her bikini top slid open under his fingers, warm breath following every inch of exposed skin.

He kissed her deeply, hands roaming lower, lifting the bottom of her bikini to reveal the smooth curve of her hip, then he pulled his throbbing dick out of his shorts.

She shivered, rolling over so she could straddle him, lining his length up with her entrance. Slowly, she lowered her wetness down on his dick.

Ramello's hands cupped her waist, steady and strong. "Damn, baby. You look so fuckin' good."

She grinned, leaning down to nibble at his jaw, fingers threading through the tight waves on his head. "You gonna make me feel good too, Daddy?"

His breath hitched as she began to move, slow, teasing, each grind sending sparks through his veins. His hands slipped beneath her, palms flat against the bare skin of her back, pulling her closer, deeper.

Dominique's lips found his, hot and wet, tongues swirling in a lazy dance as she rocked against him. The world shrank until it was just the two of them, heat, breath, and skin.

Ramello's voice was rough. "I been waitin' all day for this."

She smiled against his lips. "Me too."

With a practiced ease, he reached behind her, unclasping her bikini top and tossing it aside. His hands pressed firmly against the soft swell of her breasts, thumbs brushing over her nipples until they hardened beneath his touch.

Dominique arched into him, moaning softly as his mouth trailed down her neck and collarbone, tasting her skin.

Their bodies moved together in a slow, sensual rhythm that built and built until the air was thick with heat and heavy with promise.

Ramello's voice dropped to a growl. "You ready, baby?"

She nodded, breathless. "I'm always ready for you."

He shifted beneath her, his hands steady as he sank into her, slow and deep, both of them gasping at the sweet, searing pleasure.

Her fingers clutched at his shoulders, eyes squeezed shut as waves of sensation crashed through her.

When they finally came together, loud, desperate, and tender, it was like the whole world exploded into stars around them.

Afterward, she curled into his side, tracing lazy patterns on his chest as he held her close, the steady beat of his heart lulling her into a soft, contented silence.

"I love you," she murmured, voice thick with feeling.

He pressed a gentle kiss to her temple. "I love you too, Dominique. Always."

Wrapped in each other's arms, they let the night settle around them like a warm, protective blanket.

Home, at last.

THE MORNING SUN filtered in through the half-open blinds as Ramello slid out of bed quietly, careful not to wake Dominique. She was still sprawled across the bed, face half-buried in the pillow, one arm thrown across his side of the mattress like she could still feel him there.

He stood in the doorway for a moment, watching her. Her mouth was slightly open, curls wild and haloed around her head, the sheet clinging to the curves he'd memorized by now. A small smile tugged at the corner of his mouth before he turned and walked out, moving through the townhouse with quiet purpose.

Today was about handling business. But first…

Family.

Later That Morning

THE TABLE at the local brunch spot was loud with laughter, clinking glasses, and the kind of banter that only blood could deliver. Ramello sat at the head of the booth, one arm stretched across the top of the seat, posture relaxed, gold chain glinting in the light. His mom was seated beside him, eyes crinkled with joy as she spoke animatedly about some TV show she'd gotten addicted to. His little sisters sat across from them, tossing shade at each other over who took longer to get ready, while his younger brother, Keon, dapped him up for the third time since they got there.

"You the one actin' brand new," Keon teased. "Mr. I-been-gone-for-years now poppin' out like you the mayor."

Ramello smirked, sipping his orange juice. "Mayor? Nah. But I *am* running shit though."

"Talk your shit then, Melly," his sister, Bri, chimed in with a grin.

"Boy, hush," his mama said, though she couldn't stop smiling. "You don't need no bigger head than the one you was born with."

But she looked proud, proud in a way that made Ramello feel good, like no matter how far he'd come, this table right here would always be home base.

"I'm tryna keep y'all close," he said, looking around the table. "I want to do more for y'all. Not just money-wise. I want time with y'all. I missed too much."

"You here now," his mama said, placing her hand over his. "That's all that matters."

And that was enough for him.

A Few Hours Later

RAMELLO STEPPED out of Dominique's Range Rover, making a mental note that they would need to stop at the dealership the next day, and looked up at the house in front of him. The air smelled clean out there where he was. It was suburban — peaceful. The kind of peace money could buy.

The house was modern, two stories with high glass windows, a sleek black gate, and a long driveway that screamed security and privacy. He walked toward the real estate agent waiting near the front steps, her heels clicking nervously.

She smiled politely, trying to keep her composure, but it

was clear. By the name on the application, she hadn't expected *Ramello* to be black or to be dressed street the way he was.

"Mr. Dixon?" she said, extending a hand.

"That's me." He shook her hand.

She led him through the property, rattling off square footage, marble counters, heated floors, and the top-of-the-line security system. He nodded, asked precise questions, measured everything with the eyes of a man who thought ten moves ahead. It was a five-bedroom, six-and-a-half-bathroom house.

"You looking for something to live in or invest?" she asked casually.

"Both," he answered. "I need something comfortable for me and my wife... and solid enough to build a foundation on."

He didn't explain more than that, and she didn't ask.

By the time they circled back to the front yard, he already knew.

"I'll have my people call you. I'm interested."

Later That Afternoon

THE HOOD still smelled the same — fried food, gasoline, weed, and heat.

Familiar.

Gritty.

Alive.

Ramello kept the windows rolled down as he turned into a tucked-away block only the locals knew. The trap house didn't look like much: peeling paint, broken blinds, old Crown Vics parked out front.

But it was functioning.

He stepped out, walked up to the door, and knocked.

The door creaked open just enough to show one wary brown eye before the chain rattled loose and swung wide. The man behind it was tall and lean with a wiry frame, the kind that moved like he stayed ready for anything. He had caramel-toned skin, a low-cut fade, and a lazy gold tooth that gleamed when he smirked.

He wore a black tank top, gray sweatpants sagged just enough to show boxers underneath, and Nike slides. A pistol sat snug against his hip like it belonged there. Tattoos climbed up his neck, script, skulls, and saints, telling stories in ink.

When he saw who it was, the tension dropped instantly.

"Aww, shit. Look who finally decided to come back around," Zack greeted him.

He dapped Ramello up with the grip of someone who *knew* not to play with him then stepped aside.

"Smoke in the back. Come on in."

Weed smoke was thick in the air, loud and lingering, with the sharp bite of backwood and synthetic pine cleaner. The trap house looked like time had skipped it: warped wood floors, nicotine-stained blinds, and an old-ass couch that had definitely seen better days. But it was alive. Moving. Breathing. The walls hummed with low trap beats.

And at the center of it all sat Smoke, a heavyset man with skin the color of roasted chestnuts, dark eyes that never blinked too long, and a face that told stories no one would dare ask about. He wore a black durag under a fitted cap, an old Cash Money t-shirt stretched over his round belly, and gold grills that flashed every time he grinned. He was the kind of man who looked like he laughed easy but fought hard. Loyal to a fault. Greedy when necessary. Efficient always.

As soon as Ramello walked through the door, Smoke

stood up, arms open. "Look who done touched down like he never left."

They dapped heavy, pulling into a half-hug that said everything. No words needed.

"You already know what time it is," Ramello muttered.

Smoke nodded, glanced around, and leaned closer, brows creased in confusion. "I do?"

Ramello shrugged. "Need some fye."

One of the young niggas, maybe nineteen or twenty, had a skinny build and gold slugs in his mouth. He kept glancing at Ramello with a mix of curiosity and wariness. He sat with a Tech-9 resting on his lap, tattoos crawling up both arms like vines, and barely blinked as he smoked.

Another nigga, darker skinned with short dreads and a lean, quiet look, was bagging up on the table, moving slow and methodical, never looking up.

They didn't speak to Ramello, but they knew if he was good with Smoke, he had to be *talkin bout somethin'*.

Ramello's name still rang bells in his hood amongst the street runners of his era. The time he spent inside hadn't dulled his shine. He had no intentions of doing anything to make himself relevant to the young niggas, but he did want a strap. Prison had made him sharper, colder, more deliberate, and most of all… paranoid. Seven year in nothing but Level 5 prisons, sleeping with a knife, had him feeling naked. The world was wicked, and if he had to defend him or Dominique's life, he needed to be able to do that.

Smoke nodded, voice low. "I got what you need, big dawg. Same place."

He led Ramello to the back room where real business was handled — away from the play shooters and eyes that didn't need to see everything.

"What you need?"

"A piece," Ramello replied simply. "Nothing flashy. Something reliable."

Smoke opened a locked drawer and laid out a few options. Ramello examined them with trained eyes, checking for weight, balance, and ease of concealment. He didn't speak much. He never did when it came to business.

He chose a matte black Glock 19, checked the clip, and nodded.

"Don't ask no questions," he said, sliding the cash across the table.

"I never do."

They dapped up again, and Ramello shot out of there.

Back in the Range Rover, Ramello sat in the driver's seat, engine humming, the Glock in his lap, a black flag on top concealing it. His mind was already back on Dominique, but this, these moves, this mindset, was what made her safe. This was how he kept everything together on a solid foundation.

He was a man of strategy, love, and war.

Of family and fire.

And when he got back home, he'd be both soft and steel for the woman he loved.

That was a silent vow that he made to himself.

CHAPTER SEVEN

The townhouse smelled like home.

Savory garlic and onion sizzled in the cast iron skillet as Dominique stirred the pot with care, hips swaying slowly to the soft hum of Lauryn Hill playing in the background. Collard greens simmered on low, filling the kitchen with a comforting warmth, while seasoned chicken thighs baked in the oven, their juices crackling against the hot pan. A pot of noodles was waiting on the stove, the roux thick and creamy, nearly ready to be poured over the elbow noodles and baked until golden.

She wiped her hands on a kitchen towel, checking the cornbread in the oven before glancing at her phone. Just as she was about to start the yams, it rang.

Sierra.

Dominique stared at the screen for a beat before answering. She braced herself.

"Hey," she said, her voice soft but measured.

"Hey… you got a minute?"

Dominique leaned against the counter, wrapping her arm around herself with the phone to her ear. "Sort of. I'm in the middle of cooking."

Sierra's voice was more reserved than usual. "I just wanted to say sorry again. For real, Dom. I know I said it already, but I needed you to hear it again. I fucked up. I miss you."

Dominique exhaled. She didn't want to be cold, but the wounds were still fresh, still tender. "I appreciate that. I do. But I told you where I stand already, Sierra. I meant that."

"I know." She sighed. "I'm not tryna push nothing. I just… Can I come over? Hang out, talk? I'll bring wine."

Dominique stirred the greens absentmindedly. "I can't tonight. I'm making dinner, and Ramello's gonna be home soon. But maybe this weekend we can link. Go shopping or something."

Sierra was quiet for a second, the silence saying more than her words. "Alright. Yeah… that sounds good. Just let me know."

"I will," Dominique replied, already feeling the familiar pull of guilt. "Talk soon, okay?"

"Okay," Sierra echoed, though her voice was low with disappointment.

Right as Dominique went to say goodbye, the front door opened.

Ramello's presence hit the house like thick incense, warm, masculine, grounding. His J's padded across the floor, and she could hear the low rustle of his chain as he moved. By the time he entered the kitchen, she was still on the phone, but her attention drifted.

He looked like a whole meal himself. Dark skin glowing from the day's sun, white tee clinging to his chest, sweat still lingering from the city's heat. His eyes met hers and immediately lit with something primal.

"Who dat?" he asked, voice low and smooth as he stepped behind her.

"Sierra," Dominique mouthed, keeping her voice casual over the phone. "Yeah, I'll hit you later, aight?"

Ramello wrapped his arms around her from behind, burying his face in her neck. The scent of his cologne mixed with the spices in the air, and it made her knees damn near buckle.

"Aight, call me in the morning?"

"Okay," she said into the phone, her breath hitching as his lips brushed against her ear. "Bye, girl."

She hung up just as Ramello's hand slid down her waist and cupped her inner thigh.

"Mmm… you smell like butter and soul," he murmured into her skin. "What's all this?"

"Dinner," she managed to say, heat rising in her chest. "Mac and cheese, greens, cornbread, chicken, yams."

"Goddamn," he whispered, nibbling her earlobe. "You gon' feed me *and* fuck me? I'm blessed."

"You really are," she said with a smirk, turning to face him fully.

He grinned and leaned in, their lips meeting in a kiss that deepened quickly, growing hungry. She pressed her hands to his chest but didn't push him away.

"Lemme finish dinner first," she whispered against his lips.

Ramello shook his head, lifting her onto the counter like she weighed nothing. "Nah, lemme have a lil appetizer."

Dominique giggled, wrapping her legs around him, knowing the food would wait, but her man wouldn't.

Ramello's hands slid beneath the oversized shirt she wore, his shirt, and he groaned softly when he realized she wasn't wearing anything underneath.

"Nah, see… you disrespectful, walkin' 'round here like this," he murmured against her collarbone, dragging his tongue down to the curve of her breast. "Answerin' phones like you not sittin' on Heaven."

Ramello paused just long enough to tug her shirt over her head, tossing it carelessly behind him. Dominique's breath caught in her throat as his warm mouth found her nipple, his movements hungry — no... greedy. Her back arched, her thighs tightening around his waist. The heat in the kitchen had nothing on what he was doing to her body. She barely registered the timer going off on the oven.

"Mello..." she whispered, trying to hold on to some sense of reason. "The food..."

"Food can wait." He flicked his tongue across her nipple and kissed slow, soft circles around the other, blessing her areolas. "I'm hungry now."

He dropped to his knees between her legs, hands splayed wide on her thighs, dark eyes locked on her with worship and wickedness. His tongue dipped between her folds before she could even catch her breath, and her head fell back with a gasp.

The countertop was cool under her ass, but his mouth was fire.

"Mmm, fuck," she moaned, fingers tangling in his waves, tugging as her hips rocked into his face. "You tryna make me burn the damn house down..."

He didn't respond. He was too busy devouring her like she was the only thing that mattered. The sounds of his mouth, the wet, sinful rhythm of his tongue, filled the space louder than Lauryn Hill now. Her legs shook, her toes curled, and her free hand knocked the wooden spoon off the counter.

She was close. Too close.

But he wasn't finished.

Ramello rose to his feet, lips glistening, eyes heavy with lust. He kissed her slow and deep, letting her taste herself on his tongue before flipping her around and bending her over the counter like a ragdoll.

"You think I don't know what you do to me?" he muttered, sliding two fingers between her legs and watching her shudder. "Got me thinkin' about you when I'm supposed to be on business. Got me hard every time I walk in this fuckin' house."

She whimpered as he slid inside her slowly, filling her inch by inch until her palms pressed flat to the marble, anchoring herself.

Their moans tangled as his hips met hers again and again, each thrust deliberate, claiming, reverent.

The timer on the oven beeped again.

Neither of them moved.

"Dinner's gon' be cold," she breathed, her voice high and breathless.

Ramello groaned against her back. "It's yo fault. Stop makin' me lose my mind like this."

Her cheek pressed against the cool marble as Ramello picked up his pace, gripping her hips with a control that barely masked the way he was unraveling behind her. Each thrust shook the silverware in the drawer beneath the counter. Her breath hitched, toes curled, the sting and stretch of his dick deep in her making her eyes roll.

She wasn't quiet anymore.

"Damn, baby," she moaned, her voice hoarse, fingers slipping against the counter as he slammed into her. "You tryna fuck the soul outta me or somethin'?"

"I already got your soul," he growled, pulling her up by the throat just enough to whisper in her ear. "I'm just playin' in it."

Her knees buckled.

He caught her with one arm, spinning her around, lifting her up onto the counter like she weighed nothing. *Again.* His lips crashed against hers, the kiss messy and raw, their bodies drenched in sweat, lust, and every unspoken feeling they carried.

Then, he dropped to his knees again.

"Wait, Mello." She tried to protest, still sensitive and twitching.

But he was already spreading her wide again, licking up the mess he made her make, moaning low like she was his last meal on Earth.

She thrashed and screamed, her thighs clamping around his head, as she came so hard she knocked over the glass of sweet tea next to her elbow.

It spilled everywhere.

Neither of them cared.

Twenty minutes later, the kitchen smelled like baked chicken and sex. The candles had burned low, and Lauryn Hill had long since given way to D'Angelo crooning in the background. Dominique sat on the couch, wrapped in one of Ramello's hoodies with nothing underneath, plate balanced on her thigh.

She couldn't stop smiling.

Ramello returned from the kitchen with two glasses of juice and sat beside her, sliding his plate onto his lap. He was shirtless, boxers riding low on his hips, skin still glistening. He looked like the finest man in the south.

She nudged him with her foot. "You really a menace, bae. You coulda let me finish the damn cornbread first."

He grinned, biting into a thigh. "Shit tasted better after I tasted you."

"Boy, shut up." She laughed, cheeks aching from smiling so hard as she chewed a forkful of mac and cheese.

For a few minutes, they just ate in silence. Comfortable. Slow. Full of everything they hadn't said but didn't have to.

After the plates were cleared and her belly was full,

Dominique leaned her head on his shoulder. The TV played softly in the background, some old *Martin* rerun, but neither of them was paying attention to it.

"I'm sleepy," she mumbled.

"You should be." He smirked, kissing her temple.

She gave him a light smack on the chest but didn't move.

Eventually, Ramello pulled her to her feet, and together, they walked hand and hand to the bedroom.

She curled up against him as he reached over to turn off the bedside lamp, the room settling into darkness as they lay together in bed.

"You wild for what you did in that kitchen," she whispered sleepily.

He kissed her shoulder, eyes already heavy. "You loved it though."

"And did." She giggled tiredly.

And with the memory of everything they shared that day lingering in the sheets, they both slipped into a deep sleep, warm, fed, and in love.

DOMINIQUE ADJUSTED the heat on the stove, giving the collard greens one final stir. The sun seemed to linger behind her like a spotlight, turning the kitchen into a warm, golden cocoon. She heard Ramello and the slow, steady rhythm of his Nike slides crossing the hardwood. He walked into the kitchen and leaned against the counter with that easy, confident posture of his.

"Mmm, smells even better than it did last night," Ramello said, sniffing the air. His deep voice carried a warmth that matched the kitchen. He looked at the pot and then at her, smiling faintly. "You cooked all this just so we could reheat?"

Dominique smirked, rolling her eyes. "It's better the

second day, just like life sometimes. Don't question my methods, okay?" She set the wooden spoon down and turned to face him fully, arms crossed.

Ramello chuckled low then reached out to tug lightly at one of the loose curls framing her face. "Aight, boss lady. I stand corrected."

They shared a soft moment of silence, the kind that felt like a luxury after all the noise at the pool party the day before last, and Ramello's welcome-home party the day he got out. Dominique's mind lingered on that — a kaleidoscope of laughing faces, bustling aunties, kids running barefoot. For hours, the house had been alive with love, and she'd absorbed it like sunlight on her skin.

"Your family's something else, you know?" Dominique said finally, her tone thoughtful. "Your mom, your uncles, your cousins, and bae, your aunties? Man, they just... they were so nice. So warm. Always fussin' over you, cracking jokes, dancing, just... full of life." She glanced at him, brushing her hands on a dishtowel as she spoke.

Ramello nodded slowly, his eyes softening. "Yeah, they're something. They really love hard. That's how they are. Aunt Buck don't play bout me — and you saw how my Aunt Teka wouldn't een let me fill my own plate."

Dominique laughed. "I saw. She's got a good heart though." Then, after a beat, her voice softened. "I wished I had aunties like that."

Ramello tilted his head slightly, studying her. His smile faded just a touch. "What you mean by that?"

Dominique stiffened, her hands reflexively going to the edge of the counter. Her gaze flickered away as if the question was suddenly too heavy to hold between them. She hesitated for half a moment before shaking her head briskly and flashing a small, tight-lipped smile.

"Oh, nothing," she said, her voice lifting just enough to

sound nonchalant. She busied herself wiping away invisible specks of something on the counter, avoiding his eyes. "Just... yours are so warm, you know? Not every family's like that."

Ramello noticed the subtle shift in her tone — the way she carefully sidestepped his question, as if afraid he might uncover something she'd buried too deeply. Over the years, he'd learned bits and pieces about Dominique's past: how she'd lost both her parents in a car accident as a child and was raised by her maternal grandparents. But beyond that, she rarely opened up about her family. She had once mentioned that things with them had become somewhat strained but never elaborated. His gaze sharpened slightly, but he chose to stay silent, letting her steer the conversation away like she clearly preferred.

"Anyway," Dominique said on a lighter note, setting the dishtowel down and lifting her chin. "Spending time with your family kind of had me thinking, you know? About mine."

Ramello crossed his arms, leaning slightly closer. "Oh, yeah?"

"Yeah." She took a deep breath as if steadying herself. "I was thinking maybe I could use some of that family time. I haven't been back to Florida in over ten years, Ramello. I mean, it's just one state over, but..." She shrugged. "It feels like a world away. And after seeing you with your people the other night, I don't know. It just made me realize I've been avoiding something."

Ramello's brows lifted slightly. "You sure about that? I know you said things... ain't always easy with your folks down there."

Dominique nodded, her expression teetering somewhere between determination and vulnerability. "I know. But it's been so long. I just... I don't want to keep running, you know?" She paused then smiled softly. "Besides, we could make a trip out of it. A real trip. Hit the beach, eat some seafood, maybe even wrestle an alligator if we're feeling ambitious."

"Wrestle an alligator, huh?" Ramello said, his lips twitching into a grin.

"Hey, you just got out. Live a little," she shot back, nudging him playfully. Her smile widened, though her eyes displayed a flicker of tension beneath the surface.

Ramello studied her for another moment then finally shrugged with that easygoing air of his, like nothing in the world could rattle him. "Alright. We'll go. Florida it is."

Dominique blinked then let out an almost childlike squeal of excitement. "For real? You mean it?"

"Yeah, I mean it. How can I say no when you're over here talkin' like you're ready to tame wild animals?"

She laughed and threw her arms around him, squeezing tight. "Thank you, baby. You don't even know how much this means."

His arms came around her, anchoring her in place. "You never gotta thank me, Dominique. Not for no shit like that. Where you go, I go."

"Oh, shit!"

Ramello's brow creased in worry. "What?"

"Baby, what about your parole?"

He kissed her on her forehead. "Let me worry bout that."

Her heart swelled at that, and for a moment, she didn't think about what she'd left behind in Florida or the quiet storm stirring deep in the pit of her chest. For now, there was just this — warmth, sunlight, and the promise of going forward, wherever that was.

<hr>

"Bae!" Ramello called out to Dominique from the bathroom where he sat on the toilet, taking a shit completely naked with his boxers laying off to the side on the floor.

A minute later, Dominique appeared in the door frame of the bathroom. "What's up, baby?"

"Start packing. We're leaving tonight," he said, his attention focused on the text message he was typing.

"What? But... your parole?"

Ramello smirked, turned his phone, and showed her a cryptic message:

Cleared. 72-hour window. You owe me, nigga.

Dominique's eyes widened. "Who the fuck you know that got that kind of pull?"

"I told you... I ain't no regular nigga, baby. I got friends in all kinds of places. One of my people from the inside been eating off what I left behind. Called in a favor."

Her heart thudded. "So, we really leaving?"

He nodded. "Yeah. Early morning. Pack light. I already booked the flight under different names. Only necessities. Anything else, we'll get when we get there. We'll be in Miami tomorrow."

She looked at him in awe. "You always move like this?"

"For you? Shiiid, always." He wiped his ass and flushed the tissue down the toilet.

"Boy!"

Ramello stood and put his boxers on, flushing the toilet a second time. "What?"

"Don't nobody wanna see yo doo-doo stains!"

"Girl, hush. I done smelled yo shit for twenty-two years, and you act like you can't smell mine for five minute," Ramello said, imitating John Witherspoon's character on *Friday*.

Dominique laughed as she stood at the door, watching

him go to the sink and wash his hands before walking up to her.

He wrapped his arms around her waist and pulled her into a kiss, slow and firm. "I love you. You know that?"

Dominique nodded. "I know… I love you too."

THE TOWNHOUSE WAS QUIET, dimly lit with nothing but the moonlight spilling in through the window. Dominique had already packed the essentials, two carry-ons with their fake IDs tucked away in a zipped side pocket, and was now curled up beside Ramello on the bed. The room still smelled faintly of shea butter and cologne, the air heavy with anticipation.

They had planned to take a quick nap before their Uber came to get them. But sleep didn't come easy for Ramello. His body was still, but his mind twisted in restless circles.

He was on the beach.

Sunlight bounced off the Miami waves like diamonds. Dominique was laughing, radiant in a flowing white dress, her feet bare, curls blowing in the breeze. Ramello stood nearby, barefoot too, toes buried in the hot sand, shirt open, gold chain gleaming against his chest.

He turned to reach for her when…

Pop. Pop. Pop.

Gunshots cracked the calm. His chest exploded with fire. He fell hard, the breath knocked out of him as Dominique screamed, blood soaking the white of her dress.

"Ramello!" she wailed. But her voice was already fading, drowned out by the rush of the tide and the ringing in his ears.

He woke with a jolt.

Heart pounding. Sweat slick on his back. It was pitch dark

in the bedroom. The hum of the AC was the only sound, but everything in him was on high alert.

Dominique stirred beside him, but he kissed her temple and whispered, "Go back to sleep, baby."

Slipping from the bed in nothing but his boxers, he grabbed his phone and stepped into the hallway. The digital clock read 3:26 a.m. He scrolled down his contacts, thumb hesitating for just a second before tapping *Unc*.

The line rang twice.

"Hello." Uncle Henry's voice was thick with sleep.

"I need a favor," Ramello said, voice low but steady. "You remember that TSA chick you was talkin' 'bout at the cookout?"

"Aye, boy… the hell you doin' callin' me this late?"

"I told you, Unc. I need a favor."

Henry grunted. "What about her?"

"I need to get sum through at the airport. I ain't talkin' weed or cash. I'm talkin'… steel."

There was a pause on the line. Then, "You tryna fly with heat?"

"I had a dream," Ramello said, running a hand down his face. "And it ain't sit right with me. I don't know if it was a warning or what, but I can't go into no unfamiliar city naked. I ain't built like that."

Another pause. Then, Uncle Henry sighed. "You trust this woman with your life? You don't think she tryna set you up, do you?"

"Nah, it ain't een like that," Ramello replied. "I'm just... I don't know. You know how it is when you fresh out. A nigga just might be paranoid, but I don't like feeling like I can't protect us."

Henry exhaled, and there was some shuffling around. "Aight. I'ma make the call. But you gon' need to pick up a specific suitcase. Hard shell, dual layer. My girl know what to do with it once y'all check in. You act normal, follow the steps. Don't ask no questions. If anybody say shit, you don't know nothin'. You just flyin' to see your girl's people."

Ramello nodded, pacing now. "Bet. Text me the brand and model."

"I got you. And Ramello?"

"Yeah?"

"Move careful. Dreams ain't always just dreams, and not all the time are they accurate. Sometimes, it's your gut tryna talk before your mouth know what to say. Other times, it's just simply the universe letting you know that something bad is about to happen."

The line went dead.

Ramello stood in the hallway for a minute, letting his uncle's words sink in. Then, he turned back into the bedroom, slid back into the bed beside Dominique, and pulled her close. Her body molded to his automatically.

She didn't wake, but her lips moved against his chest. "You good?"

He held her tighter. "Yeah. Just makin' sure we both are."

CHAPTER EIGHT

The heat in Miami was different, more humid. It was the kind that kissed your skin with a sheen of sweat and made you slow down, made you take your time. As soon as Ramello and Dominique stepped out of their sleek black car, the ocean breeze wrapped around them like silk.

The valet, a young man in a crisp white uniform, rushed to open Dominique's door, his smile faltering for a half-second when she stepped out. She was stunning, and today, she wasn't trying to hide it. Her outfit was effortlessly fly: a halter jumpsuit made from sheer bronze fabric that shimmered as she moved, cinched at the waist with a designer belt. A pair of brown leather sandals with delicate gold chain straps adorned her feet, and her curls had been pinned back into a soft updo with tendrils escaping to kiss her collarbone.

Ramello stepped out the whip dressed like summer heat wrapped in confidence. His skin, rich and dark, gleamed under the Florida sun, set off perfectly by the cream short-sleeve linen button-down he wore, just a couple buttons undone to let the breeze hit his chest. The fabric was soft and expensive without screaming money, just draped easy over his broad frame.

On the bottom, he rocked olive green Tech shorts that hit right at the knee, sitting just right on his hips. They had a slight stretch to them, subtle zippers at the pockets, functional but still fly. No loud logos, just sleek and fitted. His legs were toned, clean, and oiled just enough to catch a little shine.

He had on crisp white Nike Air Force 1s, no scuffs, no creases, with matching white ankle socks. On his wrist sat a black leather-banded watch, minimal face, something classic. A pair of designer black shades hugged the bridge of his nose, shadowing his dark brown eyes just enough to keep people guessing what he was thinking.

No chain, no rings. Just his waves swimmin' and his smile shining, bright — white, and a little dangerous — cutting through the Miami heat like a damn reward.

Ramello looked like the man your daddy warned you about and your mama secretly wanted for herself. Calm. Collected. King energy on vacation.

They walked into the hotel hand in hand, and it was like the energy shifted. The lobby was grand — floor-to-ceiling windows letting in the ocean, the scent of orchids hanging in the air, and a pianist playing smooth jazz off to the side. Every employee they passed greeted them warmly but respectfully. No one stared too long, but the weight of their presence was felt.

When the concierge handed Ramello the penthouse suite keys with a "Mr. Dixon, we've prepared everything to your specifications," Dominique raised an eyebrow.

"You callee ahead?" she asked, voice low as they stepped into the private elevator.

Ramello smirked, that familiar glint in his eyes. "Hey…" He shrugged. "I do thangs."

The penthouse was everything: marble floors, a full kitchen, floor-to-ceiling views of the ocean, a private rooftop pool, and a master bedroom that looked like it was made for sin.

Dominique slipped out of her jumpsuit and into a turquoise bikini with a white cover-up knotted at one side of her hip that covered her fupa.

After she finished changing, she rifled through one of the sleek silver suitcases near the bed, looking for her sandals and a second pair of gold hoops to swap out. Her fingers brushed against something hard tucked between neatly folded T-shirts. She paused and unfolded the bulky black t-shirt.

Her heart thudded.

A gun.

Not just a little piece either.

She stared at it for a long second before picking it up carefully, her breath shallow. "Mello…" she called, her voice quiet but firm.

He stepped out of the bathroom, shirtless, towel slung low on his waist as he dried his hands. The moment he saw what she was holding, his body tensed, just for a second, but then, he walked over slowly.

"Why do you have this?" she asked, eyes never leaving the weapon. "I thought you said you wanted a fresh start. You told me you were good."

He took the gun from her gently and placed it on the bed. "I *am* good," he said. "But I'm not stupid."

She crossed her arms. "You really think we need that? Here? In *Miami*?"

He sat on the edge of the bed and pulled her between his knees, resting his hands on her hips. "Baby… I spent the last few years locked up, sleeping with a knife under my pillow every single night. That kind of survival don't just switch off. I'm not out here lookin' for trouble, but if something pop off? I need to know I can protect you. Protect *us*."

She softened slightly, fingers brushing against his shoulder. "You don't know anybody out here, babe."

"Exactly," he said. "That's why I carry. Not to flex. Not to threaten. Just in case."

There was something raw in his voice. Real. She could see it in his eyes — the weight of what he'd lived through, the paranoia that still clung to his peace. He wasn't trying to live like he was still locked up, but survival wasn't a switch you turned off just because the sun was shining and the view was pretty.

After a long pause, she nodded, leaning down to kiss his forehead. "Okay. Just… don't keep stuff like that from me. I wanna know what's going on in your head. I can handle it."

He gave her a reassuring smile, pulling her close. "I know you can. That's why you mine."

She smirked. "Damn right."

A moment passed, quiet and intimate, before she stepped back and untied her white cover-up with a playful glance over her shoulder. "Now get dressed before I take this bikini back off and we don't make it out the door."

Ramello chuckled, standing to grab his soft white shorts and a tank that hugged his muscles in all the right places.

"And bae?"

Ramello turned around. "W'sup, Mama?"

"The plane though… How'd you get the gun on the plane?"

Ramello smiled. "I told you… I do thangs."

Dominique sucked her teeth and rolled her eyes, all smiles. "Whatever."

They left soon after, heading to the upscale shops along Collins Avenue. Ramello trailed behind Dominique, watching the way her hips swayed with each step — confident, graceful, and just wild enough to make him wanna fuck her in every fitting room they passed. He loved the confidence she had in her body to still wear a two piece despite her size and weight. It was so attractive.

He had always had a thing for plus-size women: the confidence, the curves… the way they unapologetically owned their beauty. There was something about a woman who radiated elegance, strength, and sensuality all at once. He loved the way they embraced their uniqueness. Some men would disagree, but in his eyes, what was more irresistible than that?

The boutique they were shopping in was high-end and low traffic, the kind of spot where the employees were more concerned with discretion than customer service. Soft house music filled the air, and floor-to-ceiling mirrors reflected polished racks of linen, silk, and leather.

Dominique slipped behind the velvet curtain of the dressing room, a bundle of swimwear slung over her arm. Ramello stayed just outside, lounging on the built-in seat like he had all the time in the world. But the way she'd been teasing him, brushing against him, whispering slick shit in his ear, dropping her voice low and syrupy every time she asked, *"Do you like this one?"* had him sitting on the edge of his patience.

She peeked her head out the curtain. "You not even gonna help me decide?"

He looked up from his phone and smirked. "I ain't tryna get kicked up out this bitch."

She licked her lips slowly. "Then be quiet."

Ramello didn't need more than that. He pushed the curtain aside and stepped in, letting it fall shut behind him.

Inside, the air felt hotter. Tighter. Dominique stood there in a barely-there black bikini, her hard nipples protruding through the fabric, the ties at her hips hanging loose like they were just asking to be undone. Her skin shimmered under the soft golden lights, and the look in her eyes said she knew exactly what she was doing.

"Mmm," he grunted, already crowding her space. "You play too much."

"And you love it," she teased, biting her lip.

Ramello pressed her back against the wall, one hand sliding down her thigh, gripping it, lifting it around his waist. His other hand cupped the back of her neck as he kissed her, slow, deep, drugging. She moaned into his mouth as he ground against her, already hard and heavy in his shorts.

"I ain't even pull the tag off yet," she breathed against his lips.

"I'll buy it."

He reached between them and whipped his dick out, no hesitation, no warning. Dominique gasped when she felt him, thick and pulsing, sliding against her slick heat. She grabbed his shoulders, nails digging in, trying to keep quiet as he slid into her in one slow thrust that made her eyes flutter shut.

"Shhh," he whispered in her ear, voice low and delicious. "You gon' get us caught."

She bit down on her lip, nodding and breathing hard through her nose, her body already trembling as he rocked into her, slow at first, savoring it, then faster, rougher, hungry like he'd been holding back since they left the hotel.

The sound of flesh on flesh was soft but unmistakable, muffled by the music outside. Dominique clung to him, her back arched off the mirror, her breath catching with every thrust. Her leg slipped from his hip, but he caught it mid-air, never breaking rhythm.

"Damn, Melly…" she whimpered.

He grunted, jaw clenched, watching her face twist in pleasure.

"Say you mine," he growled, hips slamming into hers.

"I'm yours," she gasped. "Always."

That was all he needed. He buried himself deep one last time, groaning against her neck as he came, his breath warm and ragged. She pulsed around him, thighs trembling, her nails scraping down his back through his shirt as her own climax washed over her in waves.

They stayed like that for a moment, breath mingling, foreheads pressed together.

Then, Ramello smirked and reached for the price tag hanging from her bikini bottom.

"Told you I'd buy it."

Dominique adjusted the sheer scarf over her hair and gave herself one last look in the mirror, cheeks flushed and lips kiss swollen. Her bikini bottom sat just right on her hips now, barely clinging on, and Ramello had already tucked himself back into his shorts, face calm like he hadn't just rearranged her insides a minute ago.

"Think they know?" she whispered, smoothing down the front of the coverup she'd slipped on.

Ramello glanced at her through the mirror, running a hand over his neatly shaped hairline and flashing that innocent-ass smile, the one that had no business being on a man with that kind of stroke game.

"If they didn't know before, they gon' know when they see how you walkin'."

Dominique swatted his arm, biting back a grin. "You ain't shit."

He leaned in and kissed her neck, slow and possessive. "Nah… I'm yours."

They stepped out of the dressing room like they hadn't just risked being banned from upscale boutiques across Miami. Ramello walked ahead first, nodding casually at the sales associate near the register, cool as ever. Dominique followed, adjusting the straps of her bikini top as the woman raised an eyebrow with a smirk.

"Find everything you were looking for?" the associate asked, tone slick with implication.

"Mhmm," Dominique replied, smiling sweetly. "He bought me *exactly* what I needed."

"No bag?" the salesgirl questioned.

Ramello slid his card across the counter without flinching. "She wearin' it out."

The salesgirl laughed under her breath, rang them up, and handed over the receipt with a wink. "Well, y'all enjoy your afternoon."

"Oh, we will," Ramello said, slinging his arm over Dominique's shoulder like nothing was out of the ordinary.

As they strolled back out into the humid Miami heat, Dominique leaned into him, still glowing. "You real calm for somebody who just risked a charge in the fitting room."

He chuckled, tugging her close. "Ain't no cameras in there, baby. Just mirrors."

<hr>

THE HEAT of the sand kissed their skin as they walked hand in hand down Ocean Drive, the salty breeze swirling through Dominique's curls and fluttering the hem of her cover-up. The city was loud and alive, music bleeding from nearby patios, the scent of grilled seafood and citrus perfume in the air, but somehow, it all faded when Ramello opened the gate to one of the beachside restaurants and guided her toward a secluded table tucked beneath a white canopy.

Everything around them screamed luxury — crisp white linens, gleaming silverware, waiters in slim-cut uniforms with foreign accents, and champagne already chilling in a bucket of ice.

Ramello pulled Dominique's chair out for her then took the seat across from her, his legs spread wide, lounging like he had nothing to prove. The ocean glimmered behind him, turquoise waves curling like silk, but Dominique could hardly take her eyes off the man in front of her.

He wore light cream linen shorts that stopped just above his knee and a soft, sage green. short-sleeve button-down left halfway open, revealing the glisten of his chest and the gold chain resting against his skin. The sun brought out the gold undertones in his dark skin, and those brown eyes? Watching her like she was the finest thing he'd ever seen.

"You keep lookin' at me like that, I'ma order dessert first," he said, his voice as smooth as the waves rolling in behind them.

Dominique grinned, reaching for her water glass. "You're the dessert. I *love* chocolate"

He laughed. "I bet."

Their waiter arrived, offering a menu of fresh-caught seafood, tropical cocktails, and handcrafted pasta. At Dominique's request, Ramello ordered her a grilled lobster with garlic butter, fresh mango salad, and a frozen daiquiri. He chose the blackened grouper for himself with sides of rice, grilled corn, and topped it off with a bottle of sparkling water and pineapple juice. When the waiter walked away, Dominique leaned back, letting the ocean breeze graze her skin.

"I needed this." She sighed, eyes fluttering shut for a moment.

Ramello nodded, watching her with something deeper than lust, something warm and steady. "You deserve it."

She opened her eyes, tilting her head. "I don't think I've ever had someone take care of me like this."

"I told you I would," he replied, voice low, fingers tracing the edge of his glass. "And I don't go back on my word."

Their food arrived like art on a plate, steam curling off the lobster, the colors vibrant and fresh. Dominique moaned after the first bite — a slow, indulgent sound that made Ramello adjust himself in his seat.

"Girl," he said, laughing softly, "you better stop."

"Why?" she teased, licking a bit of butter from her fingertip. "You gon' spank me in front of the staff?"

"I'll buy this whole fuckin' restaurant and bend you over that table."

She choked on her drink, grinning, eyes dancing.

Their laughter rolled easily between them as they ate, toes buried in the sand below the table, the warmth of the Miami sun wrapping them in a soft glow. Dominique reached for his hand halfway through the meal, and he laced their fingers together like it was second nature.

Dominique sat back in her chair, her belly full and her heart even fuller. She wiped her fingers with a linen napkin and reached into her purse for her phone, glancing at Ramello with a little smile.

"I need to call my grandparents before it gets too late," she said, her voice warm, honeyed from the sun and daiquiri.

Ramello nodded, his fingers still laced in hers. "Go 'head. I'm right here."

She unlocked her phone and scrolled to "Granny & Pops" in her favorites, the two people who had given her the foundation she stood on, who had stepped in after the wreckage of her childhood and raised her with tenderness and grit. Her thumb hovered for a second before she hit the call button.

It rang once.

Twice.

"Baybeh!" Granny's voice came through the speaker, high and rich like the church songs she used to hum on Sunday mornings.

Dominique laughed. "Hey, Granny."

"Oh, I was just thinking about you, girl. You alright? You in town?"

"I am. Just got in earlier. Me and my man are out having lunch right now."

"Mmm!" Granny sang with delight. "That the same young man you was tellin' me about?"

"Yup," Dominique said, glancing at Ramello with a bashful grin. He smirked at her, chewing slowly as he watched her intently, the breeze lifting the collar of his shirt like a lover's touch.

"He treatin' you right?"

"Better than right, Granny."

"Mhmm, that's what I like to hear." Granny lowered her voice, though Pops could be heard mumbling something in the background. "You bringin' him by, or you hidin' him?"

"I wanted to stop by tomorrow if y'all around," Dominique said. "I want y'all to meet him."

"You know we always home. What time?"

"Afternoon? After lunch?"

"That's perfect. I'll fry some chicken and make your cornbread. You still don't eat pork?"

Dominique laughed. "Still don't."

"Alright, baby. Be safe. Tell your man we're lookin' forward to meetin' him."

"I will. Love you, Granny."

"Love you more."

She hung up, that familiar weight of family softening something in her chest.

"So, I get to meet the OGs tomorrow?"

Dominique nodded, cheeks still warm with emotion. "Yeah. You nervous?"

He shrugged, sipping his juice. "Nah. You already mine. They just need to see what you see."

The sincerity in his voice made her breath catch. He wasn't putting on. Wasn't pretending. He was just... him.

Solid.

Quietly confident.

Hers.

"Granny gon' love you," she said, eyes locked with his.

"I'ma love her right back," he replied.

And as the waves rolled in behind them and the sun dipped lower into the sea, it didn't feel like they were building something new.

It felt like they were remembering something ancient.

Something meant.

THE SUITE DOOR shut behind them with a soft click, sealing them away from the rest of the world. The golden hues of the Miami sunset streamed through the expansive windows, casting warm light across the sleek marble floors and white linens of the penthouse bedroom.

Dominique stepped out of her sandals at the entrance, sighing as she stretched. Her sheer white cover-up fluttered with every movement, the curves of her black bikini showing through beneath it like temptation dressed in sunlight.

Ramello was quiet, watching her from behind as he locked the door, the sound of the city muffled now by luxury and silence. His jaw flexed subtly as he took her in, long legs, sexy, mahogany skin kissed by sun and salt water, the curve of her hips accentuated by the cut of the bikini bottoms.

"You walk in front of me all day like that," he muttered, his voice low and husky, "and you really think I'm not gonna do something about it?"

She turned, smirking over her shoulder. "What you gon' do, Daddy?"

Instead of answering, he crossed the room and pulled her close, his hands gripping the back of her thighs as he lifted her effortlessly. She giggled as he carried her into the bathroom, pushing open the frosted glass door of the shower with his shoulder.

Warm water burst from the rainfall fixture above, steam rising almost immediately. He set her down gently on the black marble tiles and tugged at the string of her bikini top with slow, deliberate fingers. She returned the favor, dragging his shirt over his head and sliding his shorts down with a teasing slowness.

The water cascaded over them, washing away the remnants of sun, sweat, and salt. Ramello's hands roamed her slick, heated skin with practiced care, fingers massaging her shoulders, tracing her back, gripping her hips. Dominique pressed against him, her body pliant under his touch, her breath fogging up the glass behind them.

"You feel good out here," he murmured into her neck. "Like vacation was made just for you."

She smiled, eyes fluttering closed as he kissed her collarbone. "I needed this. You don't even know."

"I know," he whispered. "That's why we here."

They stayed in the shower longer than necessary, not in a rush, letting the steam work its way into their bones. By the time they stepped out, their skin was flushed, soft, and clean. Dominique wrapped herself in a plush white towel, while Ramello tossed one around his waist and followed her back to the bed.

The sheets felt cool against their warm skin. They collapsed side by side, bodies still damp, tangled up under the luxury linens like two secrets too sacred to tell.

Dominique rolled onto her stomach, facing him, chin resting on her arm.

"You think they'll like you?" she asked softly, referring to her grandparents.

Ramello looked down at her, smiling. "I ain't worried 'bout that. I'm me. Ain't gotta perform for nobody."

She smiled. "Good answer."

He reached over and dragged his fingers down her spine. "You excited?"

"More nervous than anything," she admitted. "It's been a minute."

He nodded. "We gon' go in there together. I got you."

There was something about the way he said *I got you* that grounded her. That eased the tension she hadn't even realized she'd been carrying all day. She leaned forward and kissed him, slow and lingering, like she was trying to say something words couldn't hold.

As night fell over the ocean and the city buzzed far below them, they curled into each other once again, safe, full, and still craving more of what they were building together.

CHAPTER NINE

THE SUNLIGHT CREEPING through the hotel curtains was soft and slow, golden warmth kissing the edge of the sheets as the city stirred beneath them. Ramello blinked awake, the deep rumble of a satisfied groan escaping his chest as his senses caught up to the sensation.

Dominique was between his legs, her full lips wrapped around him with slow, worshipful ease.

"Mmm… damn, baby…" he muttered, his voice thick from sleep, one hand lazily finding her curls as he exhaled deep and low.

She didn't stop. She just looked up at him with that same gaze that always had the power to quiet his mind — mischievous, loving, possessive. Her mouth moved with intention, slow strokes designed to keep him in the moment, not rushing toward the edge but savoring the way he twitched and gripped the sheets beneath him.

"This your good morning?" he asked through a breathless chuckle, his stomach tightening.

She pulled off for a moment and whispered, "Just want you calm and happy when you meet my people. Let me love on you real quick."

And with that, she went back down, lips and tongue moving in perfect rhythm, her hand stroking the base with practiced finesse.

Ramello let his head fall back on the pillows, letting her take her time, letting himself receive. She was good at that, knowing exactly what he needed before he even asked for it. And that shit was powerful. That was what made him keep choosing her again and again.

By the time he came, her name was a low groan at the back of his throat, and his hand was gripping the back of her head like she might float away.

Afterward, she crawled up beside him, licking her lips with a grin, and kissed him on the cheek like she hadn't just snatched his soul.

"Now, get up and get fine 'cause we got places to be," she teased, sliding off the bed and walking toward the bathroom, towel wrapped around her.

<hr>

THE AFTERNOON SUN hung warm and lazy over Miami as Dominique and Ramello turned onto the quiet, tree-lined street of her childhood neighborhood. The breeze carried the scent of mango trees, fresh-cut grass, and the familiar salt of the sea. Palm trees swayed like they were nodding in welcome, and the soft hum of Latin music floated from a nearby house.

Ramello glanced at the neat little homes lining the block, pastel blues, yellows, and corals, with bars on the windows and iron gates that had seen decades of life. Each yard told a story. Dominique pointed things out as they rolled down the street — Mrs. Ayala's porch swing, the corner where she learned to ride her bike, the house where she and Sierra used to sneak out from.

But it was the powder-blue house with the white trim and the porch filled with flowerpots that made her voice soften.

"That's it," she said.

Ramello looked over as she squeezed his hand. The front steps had fresh paint. A rocking chair creaked slowly in the breeze. Wind chimes danced by the door, and a welcome mat with two faded flamingos greeted them.

They parked and stepped out. Dominique wore a sundress that moved like water over her curves, her curls pinned up with a gold clip. Ramello had on crisp white linen pants and a sleeveless black tee that clung to his arms just enough to let folks know he didn't skip a single day in the yard. His waves were doing the usual thing, making people sick. He'd added a subtle chain but kept the rest of his fit lowkey. No need to stunt.

As they approached, the front door opened, and out stepped a woman with deep brown skin, silver and black braids tied into a bun, and gold hoops the size of saucers. Her face lit up like sunrise the moment she saw Dominique.

"There go my baby!" Her grandmother beamed, arms outstretched.

Dominique walked up the steps and melted into the hug. "Hi, Granny. I missed you so much."

Her grandfather followed behind, tall, dark-skinned, with a wide build and eyes that held wisdom, a smile threatening to break free. He walked with a cane but carried himself like a man who still knew his way around a boxing ring.

When Dominique turned and introduced Ramello, the air shifted slightly.

"Granny, Paw Paw… this is Ramello."

Ramello stepped forward, extending his hand respectfully. "Ma'am. Sir. It's a pleasure to meet y'all."

Her grandfather looked him up and down, slow and deliberate, but eventually shook his hand with a firm grip.

"Mhmm. You got strong hands. That's good. Too many soft-ass men out here these days"

"Paw Paw!" Dominique laughed, nudging him.

Her granny chuckled, already reaching out to pat Ramello's arm. "Well, look at you. Fine and polite. We like that."

They were invited in with open arms. Inside, the house smelled like comfort, fried plantains, fresh sofrito, a hint of lemon, and clean linen. Framed photos lined the walls. Dominique as a baby. School pictures. A graduation cap. One photo of a young Dominique and Sierra, grinning on a beach.

In the kitchen, a few of Dominique's cousins had already arrived. Zaria, a vibrant girl with sharp cheekbones and loud energy, gave Ramello the once over.

"So, you the famous Ramello," she said with a smirk.

Another cousin, Trey, a solid, muscular man with a gold tooth and a tank top, stood up from the table and offered a dap.

"You must be the nigga had my cousin actin' all brand new on IG," he said.

"Oh, my God." Dominique rolled her eyes. She had been on a roll posting pictures she'd had Ramello take of her since they had gotten there.

"Somethin' like that," Ramello replied with a small grin, matching his energy but not overselling it.

They sat and plates started hitting the table. Baked macaroni, yellow rice, grilled shrimp, ribs, collard greens, Dominique's grandmother had cooked like it was a holiday.

Conversation flowed, laughter rose, and Dominique leaned into Ramello's side, watching how he held his own. He wasn't loud, but his presence was felt. He spoke with clarity, answered questions honestly, and didn't flinch when her grandfather asked what he did for a living now.

"I own a few businesses," Ramello said. "Real estate. Stocks and options. I have my eggs in a few baskets."

Zaria nodded slowly, clearly impressed.

Trey, however, leaned back with a smirk. "Aight, serious question though, Melly… What's your intentions with my cousin?"

Dominique rolled her eyes. "Here we go."

But Ramello didn't miss a beat.

"My intentions?" he asked, turning to Trey. "To love her right, protect her, and build a future with her. Ain't too many women like her out here. I know what I got. I ain't playin' wit' it."

Trey studied him for a moment then nodded once. "Okay. That's solid. You say what you mean."

"I do," Ramello said. "Always."

Dominique reached over and placed her hand over his, squeezing gently. Her granddaddy watched the exchange and gave a small approving grunt.

After dinner, Trey clapped his hands and said, "Alright, y'all, skating rink night! Let's hit it."

THE AIR inside the skating rink was thick with nostalgia and neon lights. A deep red glow bounced off the glossy floor as 2000's R&B melted into trap beats over the speakers. Families and lovers skated hand in hand, while teenagers zipped by with too much confidence and not enough balance. The scent of buttery popcorn and old leather skates filled the air, mixing with bursts of laughter and the occasional screech of someone falling.

Dominique and Ramello were posted up near the benches, lacing up their skates. She wore a baby pink crop top with matching mini shorts that showed off her soft brown legs, toned and glistening. Ramello sat beside her in a crisp white tee, Nike shorts, and some fresh white socks pulled halfway up his calves. His waves were brushed down perfectly, gleaming under the lights. Even with skates on, he held that lowkey gangsta aura, confident, smooth, and quiet unless he had something to say.

"Damn, I forgot how bad these laces hurt," Dominique muttered, trying to double-knot hers.

Ramello leaned over and handled it for her, hands steady and gentle, fingers brushing her ankle. "I got you. Just stay cute."

"I was gon' do it," she teased.

"But you didn't." He smirked, leaning in to kiss her lips.

The moment felt intimate despite the chaos around them.

Soon, they were on the rink floor, wobbling at first but quickly finding a rhythm. Ramello moved slower than usual, conscious of his balance, his pride not about to let him bust his ass in front of her family.

Dominique, on the other hand, skated like she was born in a rink, spinning and gliding, looping around him and tugging him along.

Her cousins hyped her up from the sides, calling out jokes and taking shots from small bottles snuck in someone's purse.

"Y'all see Dom showin' out!" one cousin yelled.

"She got him out here lookin' like a newborn deer!" Another cracked up.

Ramello chuckled and flipped them off mid-glide. "Keep laughin', somebody gettin' tripped!"

Dominique skated back to him, lacing her fingers through his as they picked up speed together.

"Look at us," she breathed, cheeks warm. "You havin' fun?"

He looked down at her then pulled her close mid-glide. "The time of my life, bae. For real."

She rested her head against his shoulder briefly before pulling him off the floor to sit with the rest of the family.

They piled onto a row of benches near the snack area, laughing and talking over each other. Her cousins brought out a small deck of cards and started a game of Spades, dragging chairs and snack trays into a circle. The music kept rolling, the rink buzzing with life.

Ramello found himself deep in conversation with her male cousins, Dre, Lonnie, and Keem. They were older, protective, and not shy about sizing him up.

"So, you been locked up before?" Dre asked casually while shuffling the cards.

"Yeah." Ramello nodded. "Just came home this year."

It was a truthful answer without giving too much. He still didn't know them niggas.

"For what?" Lonnie asked, eyes narrowing.

"Armed robbery. Did a stretch but I ain't on that now. I'm movin' right," Ramello answered coolly, sipping a Coke.

The cousins exchanged glances. Dominique sat nearby, quietly listening.

"What you do now?" Keem followed up.

"Stocks and options mainly. Real estate. You know, always expanding and working. I handle my own shit. Don't owe nobody nothin'."

Dre nodded slowly. "You lookin' out for Mini?"

"With my life," Ramello said, tone low but serious.

That shut the conversation down in the best way.

Just as the group started laughing again and a game of Uno got passed around, the vibe changed. Dominique felt it before she saw it.

The shift in the air was immediate. Dominique went to get back on the floor when her steps slowed as her gaze locked on a familiar figure across the rink, one that pulled her back to a place she hadn't visited in years.

She didn't say a word, just turned on her heel and made her way to the edge of the rink, unfastening her skates with shaky fingers. The laughter that had filled her chest minutes ago had gone silent.

Ramello peeped it the second her light dimmed. He watched her walk off the floor and didn't hesitate to follow. He didn't need to ask; he already knew something was off.

When he reached her, she was sitting on a bench, staring down at her hands like they were a foreign language.

"Babe," he said low, crouching in front of her.

She didn't look at him. "She's here."

Ramello followed her eyes across the rink. It didn't take long to find the source.

The woman was older now, her smile hollow as she chatted with someone who clearly didn't know her story. That story.

"Her?" he confirmed.

Dominique gave a tight nod. "My aunt."

Pause.

"She the reason my mama and daddy died."

Ramello stayed quiet, letting her speak.

"They was on their way to confront her. About me. About what she let them niggas do to me. Then boom… Car crash. That was it."

She said it flatly, no emotion in her voice, but he could feel the storm building in her chest.

"I feel sick."

Ramello's jaw flexed. He stood, sat beside her, pulled her in so her thigh touched his. "Does your family know about what she did to you?"

Dominique met his eyes momentarily before looking away again. "I've only ever told one other person. Besides… this is my mom's side of the family. My aunt is my dad's sister.

He was barely able to hear her over the loud music and chatter in the rink. A part of him wanted to ask who else she could have told but decided that now wasn't the time for questions. Dominique needed comfort. There had been one other time that he had seen her shaken, and he had a nigga wacked for putting that kind of fear in his woman's heart.

He made a mental note to ask her later about who she had told about what happened to her.

"Listen to me," he said, his voice low but firm. "You not about to let that woman take one more piece of you. Not tonight."

She glanced at him, and he took her chin gently between his fingers, so she couldn't look away.

"She already took enough. Already did enough. But look at you now. Out here fine as hell, surrounded by your family, livin', thrivin', loved. You think she deserves your energy?"

Dominique blinked fast, swallowing the lump in her throat.

"You still shinin', baby," he continued, "despite all that shit. So don't let her see you sweat. You know who you are. Show her."

His words hit something deep. They didn't just wrap around her; they *held* her. Held the version of her that used to cry into her pillow. Held the little girl that was scared and silent. And she felt it. The strength he saw in her, the strength she sometimes forgot she had.

Dominique exhaled. "You right."

"I know I am." He kissed her forehead then tapped her thigh. "Come on. Let's go remind these folks who the fuck we is."

Back on the rink, it was like the mood never shifted. Her family laughed, danced, and skated under the neon lights. Dominique stepped back into the chaos like a goddess reborn, head held high, smile sharp, and eyes fierce.

Her aunt saw her. And that was enough.

No words exchanged. No scene made.

Just Dominique shining so hard it made shadows retreat.

By the time the DJ hit a slow jam, Dominique was skating backwards into Ramello's chest, giggling as he guided her across the floor with his hands on her hips. Her laughter echoed louder than the music, brighter than the lights, and every single one of her family members felt it.

THE BATHROOM DOOR eased shut behind Dominique as she stepped into the bedroom, the scent of warm cedarwood soap lingering on her skin. The soft glow of the penthouse city lights spilled through the windows, painting delicate patterns over Ramello's broad chest where she curled in close.

Her body pressed against his, warm and familiar, as she let her fingers wander over the planes of his chest, feeling the rise and fall of his steady heartbeat beneath her fingertips. Her lips traced slow kisses along the hollow of his throat, mapping out every inch like a secret only they shared. The faintest hum of his breath against her skin sent a ripple of heat through her.

Dominique's hands slid up, tangling in the hair at his nape, pulling him just a little closer until his lips brushed her temple. She pressed her body deeper into his, her hips rocking slightly with the subtle friction that made her pulse quicken.

"I needed you today," she whispered, her voice thick with emotion. "More than I knew."

Ramello's hands wrapped around her waist, fingers splaying wide, feeding her the strength she craved. He kissed the curve of her jaw, his voice low and rough with feeling. "You don't have to hold it all alone, baby. I'm right here."

Her lips found his chest again, trailing kisses down to his sternum, each one a soft declaration of love and gratitude.

Her breath hitched as his hand slid beneath the hem of her shirt, skin against skin, the warmth of him making her feel a way that words never could.

She looked up, eyes shimmering in the dim light. "I love you," she breathed, the words a delicate confession, vulnerable and raw.

Ramello's smile was slow, tender. His fingers brushed a stray piece of hair from her face before capturing her mouth in a kiss that was both fierce and gentle. Time slowed. The world outside melted away until it was just the two of them, wrapped in a cocoon of heat and whispered breaths.

His hands traced the curves of her body as they shed the last layers of clothing. She was wet, he was hard, and their skin finally met in a symphony of touch and desire. Slipping in and out of her slowly, he rotated his pelvis and dipped in it to stroke her walls, being sure to leave no spot untouched. Dominique's hands roamed over him, memorizing the strong planes of his back, the way his muscles flexed beneath her palms.

Every kiss, every caress, was a vow of safety, an unspoken assurance that here, in this space, she could be entirely herself.

Vulnerable.

Loved.

Wanted.

Their bodies moved in slow, intentional rhythm, each moment savored, each touch igniting sparks beneath the surface. Dominique's breath caught as Ramello's lips found hers again, deeper this time, his tongue tracing promises she hadn't dared to say out loud.

Tears slipped down her cheeks, not from pain but from the overwhelming release of years spent guarding herself. Here, with him, she was free to feel everything. Every touch was a balm, every kiss a healing prayer.

Ramello's voice was a low murmur against her skin, steady and sure. "You're mine. You're safe. You're loved."

Her fingers clenched into his shoulders as waves of pleasure rolled through her, a fierce and tender crescendo that left her trembling in his arms the closer she got to an orgasm. The weight she carried lifted just a little more with each heartbeat shared between them.

They came together, each of their names falling passionately from the other's lips.

Afterward, they lay tangled in quiet warmth, Dominique's head resting against Ramello's chest, listening to the steady beat of his heart, the anchor she never wanted to lose.

For the first time in a long time, she felt truly safe enough to be all the parts of herself — soft, wild, broken, and whole, wrapped in the arms of the man who loved her without hesitation.

CHAPTER TEN

THE STICKY HEAT of the strip club wrapped around Dominique and Ramello the moment they stepped inside. Dominique was in her daring black mesh dress, the sheer fabric clinging to every curve, teasing glimpses of the vibrant red bikini she wore beneath. Her heels clicked against the floor with purpose, and her hair bounced freely around her shoulders, catching the low lights as she moved. She carried a black *Chanel* clutch, and tracing the curve of her neck, a delicate gold chain, shimmering faintly with every turn of her head.

Ramello, lowkey but sharp, wore a crisp white fitted tee that hugged his broad chest, the short sleeves rolling just enough to reveal the rippling muscles of his arms. His dark denim jeans were perfectly faded, and on his feet, clean white sneakers kept the look fresh. His waves were deep and spinning atop his head.

The air was thick with the scent of cheap liquor and expensive perfumes mingling in the air. Pulsing bass rattled through the floorboards, vibrating up through their feet and into their bones.

They made their way past some of the thickest, sexiest

strippers Dade County had to offer and past a few scattered tables to their reserved section, a plush booth draped in crimson velvet shadows. The neon red and cobalt blue lights flickered overhead, casting sharp angles across Ramello's profile and Dominique's bare skin, glistening beneath the faint sheen of sweat from the Miami heat.

Ramello leaned back, flashing that bright white smile, calm, confident, unbothered by the wild energy swirling around them. He slid a crisp bill across the table to the bartender, eyes locking with Dominique's as she melted into the rhythm of the music, already feeling the night's promise.

The elevator doors hissed open and out stepped a dancer, slow, seductive, dripping with a siren's swagger. Her skin shone under the stage lights like molten bronze, her eyes heavy-lidded and dangerous, pulling every gaze in the room like gravity. She wore a barely-there red ensemble, lace and straps that left just enough to the imagination. The woman moved with the effortless sensuality of a predator.

The club DJ announced her as Sunshine, and as she climbed onto the stage, the room seemed to hold its breath. The red and blue lights sliced through the smoky haze, painting her in shadows and flames as her body twisted and dipped to *All The Time* by Jeremih. Her hips rolled like waves crashing against rocks, hands teasing the delicate lace of her outfit, lips parting in slow, breathy moans that sent a shiver through Dominique's spine.

She and her man started showering the woman in dollar bills. They intended on throwing enough to get her attention.

Ramello grinned beside her. "She gotta come to our section."

Dominique's heart quickened as they caught the dancer's eyes. The invitation was unspoken but clear. She exited the stage and weaved through the crowd. Stopping just at their table, her lips curved into a knowing smile as she leaned in close, her breath warm against Dominique's ear.

"Looks like you want more than just a show. What do you say we make this night unforgettable?"

Ramello's steady gaze flicked between Dominique and Sunshine, reading her subtle nod before he reached out, his fingers brushing Dominique's thigh possessively. They got up and followed the dancer through velvet curtains into a room pulsing with deep red lights, the world outside fading to a distant hum. The air was thick with anticipation, charged with the scent of musk, perfume, and the heat of skin.

The couple sat together on the couch, their eyes locked on the dancer as she stood before them, confidence dripping from her every move. She met their gazes with a sly grin, her voice low and sultry.

"Y'all must not be from around here," she teased, her hands resting on her hips as she swayed gently to the music.

Dominique tilted her head with a smile, leaning into Ramello. "I am, but my man isn't," she replied, her tone warm as her fingers trailed along his arm. "First summer out of prison in seven years," she continued smoothly, her voice softer now but loaded with emotion. "I wanted to make sure he has a good time — *we* all have a good time."

Sunshine's smile widened knowingly at her words, and she stepped closer to Dominique, one brow raised. "Well, lucky for y'all, I know just how to make that happen."

Dominique leaned forward ever so slightly, holding Sunshine's gaze as she pulled a few crisp blue-faced hundred-dollar bills from her purse, slipping them into the lace waistband of Sunshine's thigh-high fishnet stockings. Her fingers brushed against the smooth fabric as she leaned back with a playful smirk.

"Let's see what you got, Sunshine," Dominique said, her

pulse quickening with anticipation as the dancer's eyes gleamed with intrigue.

Sunshine leaned forward, getting close up on Dominique. Her hands were feather-light at first, tracing delicate paths along Dominique's exposed shoulders, fingers dipping beneath the sheer cover-up to brush warm skin. Dominique shivered, lips parting as the dancer's mouth ghosted over her collarbone, sending sparks racing down her spine.

Ramello's fingers found the ties of Dominique's cover-up, slowly pulling it free to reveal the curves beneath. His lips followed, planting slow kisses along her neck, down to the swell of her breasts, thumbs teasing the soft peaks until Dominique gasped and arched into him.

Ramello's mouth found hers then, slow and demanding, tongues dancing in a heated tango as his hands roamed boldly over every inch of her skin, worshipping and claiming. Dominique's fingers rubbed through his waves, pulling him closer, her body burning for more.

Sunshine knelt before Dominique, her hands sliding along her thighs and her lips teasing tender skin. Gentle at first, she began flicking her tongue and kissing along Dominique's inner thighs, her movements slow but deliberate, sending tremors of pleasure that left Dominique trembling.

Ramello shifted then, his strong hands guiding Dominique and Sunshine to create a seamless flow of move-ments. He eased himself down onto the couch, leaning back, his broad frame radiating a commanding energy. His intense gaze followed Dominique as she climbed onto his lap, her movements fluid and sensual, straddling him with ease.

As her lips claimed his in a fiery kiss, Sunshine lingered beside them, her soft hands finding their way to the hem of Ramello's shirt. Dominique's fingers joined, tugging the fabric upward while Sunshine's touch trailed his skin, making him shiver with every glide of her nails. Together, they peeled away his shirt, revealing his sculpted chest. Dominique leaned back for just a moment, her lips curving into a slow, appreciative smile, before she dived back in, her kisses fierce against the side of his jaw, her teeth grazing along the stubble above his neck.

Sunshine moved lower, fingers working the fastening of the belt and button of his jeans as Dominique shifted, helping to ease them down over his hips. Ramello groaned, his hands still steady on Dominique's waist, one sliding up her back as if to pull her closer. Sunshine, now on her knees, slid his jeans the rest of the way off, her palms caressing his thighs. She glanced up, her lips brushing along Dominique's shoulder in a silent exchange of heat and rhythm.

As Dominique kissed his neck, her breath hot against his skin, Sunshine's hands gripped his full length, her touch making him grow even harder. Ramello let himself sink deeper into the couch, his head tilting back as the dancer's hands wrapped delicately yet firmly around his shaft. Her strokes were slow and purposeful, building desire with every rhythmic motion. Dominique's hands slid along his broad chest, her fingertips exploring the firm planes of his muscles as her lips never left his skin, kissing and biting in a fevered attempt to drive him wild.

Moments later, Sunshine took Ramello into her mouth, warm, wet and teasing, her tongue working with expert skill as she built him closer and closer toward release. Dominique's hips rolled against him, her heated body pressing into his chest as her hands laced into his hair, holding him against her as they kissed passionately, Sunshine bobbing her head in his lap behind her. Ramello groaned into her kiss, his body overwhelmed by the sensations of lips, hands, and tongues worshipping him in unison.

Sunshine paused briefly, releasing Ramello from her mouth with a slow, teasing kiss on the mushroom shaped tip of his dick before rising to retrieve a condom from a nearby bowl. She returned, skillfully rolling it over his length, then eased herself onto his lap. Straddling him, her movements were rhythmic and deliberate as she eased down on him. Her hips rolled with slow, fluid intensity, igniting a chorus of blissful moans. Ramello's hands searched for her waist to guide her as she set the pace, but only found Dominique, leaving his connection to Sunshine primal and electric. Sunshine's lips pressed against Dominique's neck and shoulders, her kisses intensifying the intimacy while she rode him with a passion.

Dominique, still pressed close, drank in the scene through hooded eyes, her hunger mounting. Her lips resumed their exploration of Ramello's jawline, trailing kisses down to the column of his throat, the symphony of moans and ragged breaths weaving a melody around them.

Then, with a heated whisper, Ramello shifted his attention back to Dominique. Pulling her up, his lips brushed her ear, his voice rough with desire. "Come here, baby." His tone was a sultry command. "Sit on my face… let Daddy taste you."

His words made her even more wet than she already was, and with a knowing smile, Dominique slid closer, the fire between them reaching a fever pitch.

Her breath hitched, anticipation coursing through her as she shifted, got up, and settled down over Ramello's eager mouth. He raised her mesh dress up to her waist and pulled her panties to the side. Sunshine continued to ride him below as his tongue teased and explored Dominique's folds, his hands roaming her back and hips. They had shifted so that Ramello was lying flat on his back.

Dominique moaned, losing herself in the exquisite sensation of being both taken and pleased, wrapped in the heat and rhythm of their erotic dance. A few minutes later, Dominique came hard, soaking Ramello's lower face in her juices.

Breathless and flushed from the heat of the moment, Dominique gently slid off Ramello's mouth, a satisfied smile playing on her lips. Sunshine slowed her movements, giving Ramello just enough time to steady his racing heart.

Dominique caught her breath and glanced toward the bar. "I'm gonna hit the bathroom," she said, pulling her dress down and brushing a stray curl from her face.

Ramello nodded, his gaze heavy with promise. "Be careful, baby."

Sunshine got off of his dick and went back to sucking him.

Dominique weaved through the crowd, the sticky heat of the club clinging to her skin as neon lights painted everything in deep reds and blues. She felt the bass thump in her chest, a reminder of the wild night unfolding.

As she turned down a dimly lit hallway, she thought she caught a flicker of movement out of the corner of her eye, a familiar silhouette standing just beyond the glow of the club's neon. Her breath caught.

"Sierra?"

But when Dominique blinked, the shadow had vanished. She shook her head, telling herself she must be imagining things. The club's haze and alcohol were playing tricks on her.

Still, a quiet knot of unease settled in her stomach as she stepped into the cool bathroom, locking the door behind her. She splashed water on her face, blotting gently with a towel, trying to center herself before returning to the chaos waiting outside. She looked up into the mirror, checking her appearance, before taking a deep breath, steadying herself before stepping back out into the pulsing heat of the club. The neon lights flickered like fireflies, the music vibrating through the floor beneath her feet. She moved toward the private section, eager to get back to Ramello and the dancer.

As she approached, the sight before her mesmerized her.

Ramello's head was tilted back against the couch, his eyes shut, jaw slack, lips softly parted as a slow, rumbling groan escaped his throat. Sunshine was on her knees in front of him, her dark hair cascading over her shoulders as her lips worked up and down his thick length. Her tongue licked and teased at every sensitive spot, her hands stroking at the base in perfect rhythm with the motions of her mouth.

Dominique stood frozen in the doorway, in awe at the sight before her. She hadn't meant to stop — hadn't planned to stand there, silently watching — but something about the scene pulled at her, rooting her to the spot. Her chest rose and fell in quick, shallow breaths as she took it all in — the flicker of Ramello's muscles as he shifted beneath the dancer's touch, the almost indecent wet sounds of her tongue, and the restrained growl vibrating from deep within Ramello.

Her eyes traveled over him, his tensed thighs, his hand resting on the back of the dancer's head. His fingers flexed, gripping her hair tighter as he pushed her down farther onto him, fucking her face. Dominique knew that touch, knew that control. She swallowed hard, heat pooling low in her belly.

And then it happened.

Ramello's eyes fluttered open, dark and piercing, and they locked on hers.

Dominique's breath caught in her throat, her heart hammering as an illicit thrill surged through her. There was no shock in his expression, no startle at her presence — just a sharp, deliberate hunger. That look sliced right through her, leaving her breathless. His lips curled into the faintest hint of a smirk, as if he knew exactly what this was doing to her.

The ache between Dominique's legs intensified, an uncontrollable wave of arousal washing over her. She could feel it — feel the way her panties dampened with heat and need as her body responded. Her nipples tightened against her bra and shirt, hard and sensitive, almost painfully so. She crossed her arms over her chest instinctively, as if hiding the reaction, but it was no use — her whole body was alight, humming with the excitement of watching her man unravel under someone else's touch.

Ramello groaned again, louder this time, his body betraying how close he was. He kept his eyes on Dominique, his hand guiding the dancer's pace as she took him deep, her moans vibrating along his length. The dirty, intimate sounds filled the room, and Dominique couldn't stop herself from leaning against the wall slightly for support, her thighs clenching together in a vain attempt to relieve the pressure building inside her.

Her gaze drifted to Sunshine, to the way her tongue slipped out, swirling over his tip before taking him deep again, her cheeks hollowed with effort. The sight was obscene, raw — and beautiful in a wild, untamed way that only made Dominique's need burn hotter. She bit her lip, unable to tear her gaze away as Ramello's breathing quickened, his abs tightening, his hand fisting Sunshine's hair as he thrust his hips into her mouth.

"Fuck," he hissed, his jaw clenching, his gaze still locked on Dominique.

She couldn't look away. Even if she wanted to, she wouldn't. Her heart pounded in her chest as electricity crackled through her veins. She felt vulnerable, exposed, but she was more turned on than she could ever remember, her desire unmistakable, undeniable.

Ramello finally broke, his body tensing as his head fell back, a deep, guttural groan escaping his throat. "Oh, shit. I'm cummin'. I'm fuckin' cummin'."

Sunshine didn't stop, her movements intensifying, taking him deeper as he filled the tip of the condom up to capacity.

Her lips clung to him, milking every last ounce of pleasure from his body as he sagged against the couch.

And still, Dominique stood there, heat flooding her cheeks as her thighs pressed together harder now, powerless against the arousal pulsing through her. Finally, Ramello's gaze returned to hers, a knowing, satisfied look in his eyes. That small, wicked smirk returned, as if he could see the thoughts running through her mind.

Dominique exhaled slowly, not trusting herself to move, her lips slightly parted. She wanted to walk away, to compose herself, to pretend she hadn't just been utterly captivated, turned on, undone by it all. But her body said otherwise. It screamed at her to stay, to let her legs carry her to him, to touch him, to give in to the intoxicating mix of jealousy and desire burning inside her.

And the worst part — the part that thrilled her most — was that Ramello seemed to know it.

Ramello looked up, his smile raw and real. "You good?" he whispered.

"I'm amazing, Daddy. You good?" she moaned.

"I'm good as fuck, baby." Ramello kissed her.

Sunshine stood with a smile, sauntering over to a small dresser tucked against the deep red walls of the dimly lit private room, rummaging through it before pulling out a wipe. With a graceful flick of her wrist, she tore it open and wiped her mouth. Sliding on a pair of latex gloves, she grabbed another wipe before turning her attention back to Ramello. Lowering herself gracefully in front of him, she carefully removed the soiled condom and cleaned his shaft, balls, and mushroom tip.

She stood and turned to dispose of the condom–

"Aht, aht…" Dominique said.

She turned back toward them, to find Dominique going in her purse, removing some Kleenex. "I'll take that."

Sunshine smiled, before handing the condom over. "Sure."

"Thank you very much." Dominique wrapped the used condom in tissue and zipped it into a compartment inside her *Chanel* clutch.

"Well, aren't you the careful one," Sunshine said.

"Mhmm." Dominique gave a head nod.

Sunshine's smile widened into something almost playful. "Well, anyways, That was fun," she purred, her voice velvety smooth, carrying a hint of mischief. Her gaze lingered on Ramello for just a second longer, as if to silently savor the memory. Then, she shifted her attention to Dominique, giving her an equally lingering look. "If y'all are ever back in town, make sure you come find me. I'll make sure we have… another unforgettable night."

She winked as she stepped toward the door, her heels clicking softly against the polished floor. Pausing briefly with her hand on the doorknob, she tossed a final glance over her shoulder. "Until then, stay wild." And with that, she disappeared, leaving the faintest scent of her perfume lingering in the air behind her.

For a moment, the room was quiet.

"'Stay wild', huh?" Ramello echoed, chuckling like he couldn't quite believe the night they'd just had. He looked at Dominique, his gaze softening but still carrying that ever-present glint of amusement.

Dominique glared at him for a beat, but her lips twitched, threatening a smile she tried to fight back. "Boy, get dressed so we can go!"

<hr>

Morning light filtered softly through the half-open curtains, casting a warm glow over the penthouse. Ramello stirred slowly, eyelids heavy but reluctant to open. The quiet hum of the city outside was a distant murmur compared to the vibrant pulse of last night's memories still flickering behind his eyes. He turned his head and caught sight of Dominique, still curled against his chest, her breathing even and peaceful.

Last night felt like a break from the world, a stolen moment where pleasure and connection wiped away the grime of the streets and the cold reality others like him often faced.

He closed his eyes again, replaying the night, the way Dominique's laugh echoed through the club, the hypnotic pull of Sunshine's touch, the way he felt as he locked eyes with Dominique as he came in the dancer's mouth.

He traced a finger along Dominique's arm, whispering softly, "Rise and shine, sexy."

The bed shifted as she stirred awake, her eyes meeting his with sleepy clarity. She smiled and stretched, no words needed.

Outside, the Miami sun climbed higher, bathing the city in gold.

"Oh, shit. I done left my damn… Baby, I'm finna shoot downstairs to the car. I done left my phone in that mufucka." He kissed her cheek. "Be right back."

"Okay," she said. "Oh, bae."

Ramello stopped just as he reached the door. "W'sup, bay?"

"Can you grab me a orange juice on the way back?"

"You know I got you."

Ramello left, closing and locking the door behind him, and Dominique's phone buzzed as if on cue. Seeing Sierra's name flashing on the screen stirred a mix of emotions she wasn't ready to face, and she debated whether to answer.

Finally, she swiped up on the green button. "Sierra."

"Dom, can we talk?" The voice was softer than she expected, tinged with a hesitant vulnerability.

"I've been busy," Dominique replied cautiously.

"Yeah, I know." Sierra's tone sharpened. "You really out here having fun in Miami?"

Dominique's brow furrowed. "How do you know I'm in Miami?"

There was a pause before Sierra admitted, "Lonnie posted it on his IG story. You were in the background at that party."

Dominique felt a pang but said nothing about how she'd thought she caught a glimpse of Sierra herself somewhere unexpected. Instead, she kept her voice steady. "So, you've been watching."

"I'm just trying to check on you," Sierra said, frustration creeping in. "But honestly, the way you're acting, it's exactly what I said was going to happen."

Dominique's patience thinned. "Sierra, I'm living my life. You can't keep holding on to this anger and resentment."

"Anger? Resentment? You shut me out first," Sierra fired back. "I'm trying to look out for you, but you don't wanna listen."

Dominique shook her head, ready to end it. "Not now."

Before she could hang up, Sierra's voice softened, almost whispering, "I thought I saw you last night… at the club."

Dominique's heart skipped. She remembered it too, that moment of recognition she hadn't dared to speak aloud. But she kept it inside, not ready to bring suspicion into their fragile peace.

Dominique's fingers trembled slightly as she ended the call. Sierra's words echoed in her mind. *"I thought I saw you last night… at the club."*

She sat back, the noise of Miami's heat and the distant waves feeling suddenly heavy in the quiet of the room. *Did I really see her?* The memory flickered, a shadow, a familiar silhouette just out of the corner of her eye.

Why didn't I say anything? Part of her wanted to confront it head-on, to demand answers. But another part, the part that had learned to protect herself, held that secret close, burying it deep beneath layers of caution. She didn't want to drag Ramello into this yet — not when they were having so much fun.

Maybe I'm just paranoid. Maybe it was someone else. She forced the thought down, but the knot in her stomach tightened. Swiping her screen, she went to the settings in her phone and turned off her location. Dominique took a deep breath, trying to steady herself. *Keep enjoying this trip. Keep moving forward. I'll deal with Sierra when the time comes.*

For now, she busied herself with thoughts of the hot Miami day and the false comfort of distraction, but the question lingered, unspoken and heavy.

Had Sierra followed her to Miami?

CHAPTER ELEVEN

Later that day, while Dominique and Ramello were out shopping, one of her older cousins, Dre, hit her line and insisted they pull up to the family BBQ that was already in the works.

Dominique laughed. "Didn't we just eat together the other day?"

"We celebratin' you," he said over the phone. "We missed you. Come eat, laugh, be loved on. That's it."

"Awww."

Dominique didn't argue. She felt the weight of the past still lingering in her chest, but the thought of being surrounded by people who had watched her grow up, who had her back, brought her a small wave of comfort. Plus, Ramello deserved to experience more of her world when it wasn't heavy with shadows.

So, they pulled up, fresh, sun-kissed, and matching in black and white like they hadn't just spent the last week riding emotional highs and lows. This was a reset. A reminder. Family first. Healing second. Good food and a little Hennessy somewhere in the mix.

The backyard was already full, kids running wild, uncles

slapping bones on the Spades table, old-school R&B riding the breeze, and the smell of seasoned meat thick in the air. Charcoal smoke danced with laughter and gossip.

As soon as Dominique and Ramello stepped through the gate, Lonnie was the first to spot them. He shot up from his chair and walked over, holding a red cup in one hand, his gold fronts catching the sun. "Ayyye! There they go!"

"Don't start." Dominique laughed, wrapping her arms around her cousin as he pulled her into a tight hug.

"I ain't say nothin'!" He grinned. "But I see y'all. Y'all glowin' and shit, lookin' like vacation money and premium coconut oil."

Ramello smirked and dapped him up. "Good to see you again, man. Fasho."

"Y'all came just in time," Dre called from the grill, flipping ribs with one hand and puffing on a blunt with the other. "We was bout to say grace, but I told 'em we was waitin' on Mini and her man."

Dominique's grandparents were sitting on the porch under the shade, big fans in hand. As she approached, her grandmother gave her that look, the one that said *I saw what happened, but you safe now.* Her grandfather stood to give Ramello a handshake that turned into a one-armed hug.

"Good to see you again, young man," he said with quiet strength. "Y'all eat somethin' yet?"

"We're about to," Dominique said, grateful to slide back into the familiar rhythm of family.

Plates were made, drinks poured, and folding chairs unfolded in circles. Ramello held his plate like a man at peace, devouring the ribs and baked mac like he'd been eating from the family's table for years. Dominique watched him laugh with Dre and Lonnie, joining in their shit talking like he belonged there all along.

But not everyone was settled just yet.

A quiet murmuring started near the driveway, and Dominique's body stiffened as she looked up and saw a familiar face. Sierra. She looked at Ramello, who was completely taken back, brows creased in disbelief, probably thinking the same thing everyone else was.

This bitch is crazy.

She wasn't dressed like she came to stir trouble. She looked casual, hair in a bun, eyes searching. A few heads turned and stayed turned. No one had invited her, and no one was quick to welcome her either.

Dominique didn't move. She didn't flinch.

It was Lonnie who approached first, shoulders tense, voice low. "Yo, what the fuck are you doin' here?"

Sierra's eyes flicked to Dominique, then her grandparents, and then back to Lonnie. "I just came to speak."

"You coulda called," he said. "You ain't welcome here."

"I just came to talk to Domo. That's it." She took a step forward, nodding at Dominique.

Dominique crossed her arms. "You don't have the right."

"I don't?" Sierra's voice rose with disbelief. "After everything I held for you? Everything I protected you from?"

Dominique didn't move. "I didn't ask for that. And I damn sure didn't ask for you to show up here."

Sierra's eyes darkened. "Nah, see, you not about to act brand new. Not after I carried your secrets for *years.* When your aunt was letting grown-ass men touch and fuck on you for *crumbs* of crack, who was there?"

The crowd gasped. Someone's plate dropped.

Dominique's jaw clenched, her breath coming in fast, shallow huffs.

Sierra wasn't done. Her voice cracked but turned venomous. "And when you *finally* broke down and told your parents the truth? When you *finally* said what that bitch was doin' to you… They left the house *screaming.* Speeding down the highway. Crying. Ready to kill that bitch. *And they died.* They died tryin' to save you from something *you* let happen for *years!*"

Dominique froze, the air sucked from her lungs, and time went still.

"You wanna act like I'm the villain now?" Sierra continued, her voice wild and unhinged. "When I'm the one who held you through the worst of it? I *loved* you! And you treat me like shit because I hurt your fuckin' feelings?"

That was it.

Dominique lunged. Her fist met Sierra's jaw with a sharp crack, and before Sierra could react, Dre and Lonnie's girls, along with a few more of her cousins, were on her too.

"You stupid ass ho!"!"

"Disrespectful *bitch!*"

Chairs were flipped. Drinks were spilled. And Sierra was screaming, trying to swing back, but she never stood a chance.

Together, Dominique and her family beat Sierra down. Punching, kicking, stomping, and dragging her all over the yard for showing up at their grandparents' house and disrespecting them in such a way.

Ramello moved fast, not to jump in but to pull Dominique away, wrapping both arms around her waist and anchoring her to his chest.

"Let me go!" Dominique screamed, struggling to free herself from his grasp.

"Nah, bae," he whispered against her ear. "You got her already. You did what you had to do, baby. You good now."

She was shaking, her eyes wild, her breath ragged, but slowly, she stopped fighting.

Meanwhile, Dre's wife dragged Sierra to her car at the end of the driveway by her hair, her face bloody and her voice hoarse from screaming.

"I *was* your sister!" Sierra shouted as she flailed around, trying to free herself from the vice grip on her hair. "I held you when you had *no one!* I loved you more than anybody!"

Angela, Dre's wife, punched Sierra in the face one last time. "Don't speak to her, bitch! Get the fuck up outta here."

Dre followed his wife out to the driveway and slammed the gate behind him. He and Angela made sure that Sierra left without further issues.

Silence followed shortly after.

Then, Granny stood up and, without a word, turned the music up louder. A slow, old-school groove filled the backyard again. Dre went back to the grill, acting like the whole damn explosion hadn't just happened. Lonnie grabbed a fresh cup of Hennessy, and the kids resumed their water gun fight like nothing happened.

Dominique was still in Ramello's arms, trembling.

Her grandmother came over and laid her hand gently on her cheek. "It wasn't your fault, Dominique. You know that, right?"

Dominique shivered and nodded.

"I knew all along."

Dominique looked up, disbelief written all over her face.

"Your mother called me, screaming in a rage the day of the car crash, telling me what she was about to go do to your father's sister and why." She began rubbing Dominique's back. "You were a child, Dominique. What happened to them ain't your fault. What happened to *you* wasn't your fault. None of it was."

Dominique nodded, tears slipping silently down her cheeks, not from shame but from release.

And as she stood in the center of her family, bruised but upright, protected and *seen*, she realized something. She was finally free and surrounded by a love that would never use her pain against her again.

Ramello leaned in close to her ear again, brushing a kiss behind her earlobe. "Still shinin', baby. That bitch ain't did a damn thing."

DOMINIQUE LEANED against the porch railing, watching her cousins play Spades at the folding table under the string lights. Her heart felt full, but her mind drifted.

Sierra.

That name used to feel like home. Now, it left a weight on her chest. It wasn't just the argument. It wasn't even just the jealousy. It was everything that came before all of that.

Sierra had always been complicated. Brilliant but wild, loyal until she wasn't. Dominique's grandparents had taken her in when no one else would, fed her, clothed her, treated her like family when the system had failed her. But as they all got older, Sierra started acting out. Stealing. Lying. Disrespecting the same people who saved her. The final straw had come when Dominique's grandparents caught her sneaking men into the house, disrespecting their rules and their generosity.

She had cursed out Dominique's grandfather, called him everything but a child of God, and then disappeared for weeks. When she came back, it was with an attitude and excuses but no remorse. Dominique had tried to make peace between them, tried to be the bridge. But Sierra had set fire to it. From then on, the family was done with her. No one said it out loud, but the message was clear.

They didn't fuck with her anymore.

Dominique never told Ramello all of it. She barely told herself. But the look in her family's eyes whenever Sierra's name came up said enough.

So, when she thought she saw her that night in the strip

club, just a flicker of familiarity in the corner of her eye, it wasn't just paranoia. It was fear. Because Sierra didn't just represent drama... She represented a part of Dominique's past that tried to unravel everything she had fought to build. Hence, the reason she left Miami in the first place. Sierra, having nothing left in Florida anyway, simply tagged along. They got their first apartment and made a living for themselves in Georgia.

She had left a part of her in Florida back then, a piece that Ramello's love had given her the power to face after over ten years. She didn't know what had made him suggest they visit, but she was glad he did.

As the sun dipped lower in the sky, the backyard buzzed with the kind of golden-hour magic that only Black family barbecues could conjure. The speakers hummed with the sounds of old Frankie Beverly & Maze, kids were crashing from sugar highs, and the grown folks were leaning back in their chairs, bellies full and hearts even fuller.

Dominique sat on the edge of the porch, a styrofoam plate of peach cobbler in her lap, her bare feet brushing the cool grass beneath. She had slipped out of her heels hours ago, hair now tied up in a silk scarf one of her aunties had handed her mid-party. The wind was soft, her soul lighter.

Ramello approached from the grill area, wiping his hands on a paper towel before plopping down beside her. His all-black tee clung to his chest, the scent of smoke and cologne lingering around him. Without saying a word, he took her plate and scooped a spoonful of cobbler into his mouth.

She squinted at him. "You really just gon' eat my last bite?"

He licked his lips, smirking. "You wasn't eatin' it fast enough."

"Greedy ass." She laughed, playfully nudging his knee with her own.

They sat there for a beat, just watching the sky fade into pinks and purples. The laughter behind them was distant now, like background music to a more private moment.

Ramello leaned his head against hers, his voice low and soft. "Yo people love you. You know that, right?"

She nodded slowly. "I know. I just forgot for a minute. Been carrying so much alone for so long, it's like I didn't leave room for any of this."

He reached for her hand, locking their fingers together. "You ain't alone no more, baby. Not in any way."

Her eyes glistened, not enough to cry but enough for him to see the emotion brimming beneath the surface.

"I felt that today," she whispered. "The way you held me down, the way my family been loving on me... I ain't felt this safe in years."

He kissed her temple. "That's how it's supposed to be. You protect the ones you love. You build with 'em. You show up, even when it's hard."

Dominique turned to him and wrapped her arms around his neck, her face tucked into the crook of his shoulder. "I love you," she said, voice muffled into his skin. "I love you *so* much, Ramello."

He held her close, one hand on her waist, the other smoothing over the curve of her back. "I love you more, baby."

And in that moment, with the smell of grilled meat still in the air, the sound of kids laughing in the distance, and the last bit of sunlight kissing their skin, they were both reminded that love, real love, wasn't always loud. Sometimes, it was just a quiet seat on the porch, a shared plate of cobbler, and the kind of silence that said. "We're in this together."

That night, Dominique and Ramello packed the last of their bags. The Miami breeze whispered through the open doors, carrying with it the salty promise of freedom and new beginnings.

Dominique watched as Ramello's folded a crisp shirt, his eyes calm. This trip had been a taste of the life they wanted, a glimpse of a future full of sun, laughter, and family.

"This trip was A1. Too bad we can't stay forever. Now, it's time to go home to my parole stuff and get our affairs in order. We need to set the foundation before we can really build the life we wanna live."

Dominique nodded. "I know. But we'll get there. Together."

He smiled, that bright, confident smile she loved. "Yeah. We're gonna build something solid. For us. For them. For our future."

Dominique stepped closer, pressing her forehead to his. "You ready?"

Ramello's dark eyes met hers, unwavering. "For you? Always. For this? We'll make it work."

As they zipped the last of the bags closed, the two shared a quiet moment, a deep breath between worlds. Miami had given them joy, escape, a glimpse of sunlit dreams. Now, home awaited, the streets that had shaped Ramello's strength, the family that fueled his heart, the responsibilities he was ready to claim.

The future was uncertain, but their bond was unshakable.

And together, they were unstoppable.

CHAPTER TWELVE

THE FOLLOWING DAY, the airport buzzed around them. Luggage wheels dragged across glossy floors, the echo of gate announcements, babies crying somewhere in the distance. But for Dominique and Ramello, the noise faded into background static.

They stood side by side in the TSA line, fingers laced together. Ramello had one hand on her lower back, thumb brushing slow circles through her shirt. They were exhausted but happy, their bodies still warm from the penthouse morning, from whispered I love yous and playful arguments over who packed what. Miami had changed them.

"I think I wanna go back next month," Dominique said softly, eyes on the conveyor belt ahead.

Ramello smiled. "Shit, I was thinkin' the same thing."

She leaned into him, pressing her lips to his shoulder. "I like us like this."

"I like us always."

But the tender moment was pierced by a security guard's raised voice.

"Ma'am… excuse me… MA'AM!"

The energy in the terminal shifted. Subtle. Like the air had dropped ten degrees.

Another officer's voice joined the first. "She's got a weapon! Lock down this concourse now!"

Dominique looked up, brows furrowed.

And that was when she saw her.

Sierra.

Hair wild. Face smeared with tears and mascara. Eyes locked straight ahead like she couldn't see anything else but them.

She was screaming something, but it was drowned out by the panic swelling behind her — people turning, gasping, pulling children close.

Officers shouting commands.

Then…

"RAMELLO!"

Sierra's voice tore through the chaos like a jagged knife.

Dominique didn't have time to scream. To move. To breathe.

Sierra let out one last sob as she raised her gun and pointed it in Dominique's and Ramello's direction.

POP.

POP.

She let off two shots right as she was tackled by three TSA officers, then the gun clattered to the ground, sliding toward a line of screaming passengers. Ramello's body jerked back. Blood bloomed through his white shirt, and he fell to the floor bloody.

Dominique's scream shattered the air. "No! Ramello!"

"I loved you!" Sierra shrieked as she fought the officers piled on top of her. "You were mine before you met him! You were always mine! How could you forget about me!"

Her cries faded beneath the weight of bodies holding her down.

Dominique dropped beside Ramello, her hands shaking as she pressed them to his wound.

"Stay with me," she begged, panic clawing at her throat. "Please stay with me."

"I'm… I'm alright," he whispered, teeth clenched through the pain. "I–I'm… bae."

Blood soaked into her jeans. Her hands. Her soul.

Sirens blared inside the terminal. Medics rushed through the chaos. Orders were barked into radios. Bystanders filmed on their phones. Somewhere in the world, an ambulance could be heard approaching, and eventually, it arrived. Ramello was being loaded onto the gurney by EMT workers when Dominique tried to stand and stumbled instead.

Everything around her went fuzzy.

The world spun.

Then her body gave out.

THE SHARP SCENT of antiseptic clung to the air as machines beeped steadily around Dominique. Her lashes fluttered open slowly, the sterile ceiling above her blurry through the haze of anxiety and exhaustion.

For a moment, she couldn't remember where she was.

Then, it all crashed back — the echo of Sierra's voice, the flash of the gun, Ramello's body dropping beside her like dead weight, the chaos erupting at the airport. She had screamed, tried to hold him, but the blood… It was too much.

Her chest tightened.

A nurse appeared at her side. "You're awake," she said gently. "You passed out earlier from shock and dehydration. But your vitals are steady now."

Dominique sat up too quickly, ignoring the nurse's protests. "Where's my man? Where's Ramello?"

"He's stable. Surgery went well. He's in recovery."

"Can I see him?"

The nurse hesitated. "You should rest, but… I'll see what I can do."

Dominique wasn't waiting. The moment she was left alone, she pulled the IV from her arm, still dizzy but fueled by sheer will. Her bare feet padded down the cool hallway floors until she reached a dry erase board with patients' names and room numbers. Scanning it until she found the name *Dixon,* she made her way to his room with urgency. There, she pushed open the door slowly.

Ramello lay still, his shoulder heavily bandaged, color slowly returning to his face. One arm was across his chest, the other in a sling. His eyes fluttered open as the door clicked shut.

"Dominique?" His voice was rough, but when he saw her, his whole face softened.

She rushed to him and pressed a kiss to his forehead, her hands trembling. "Don't you ever fucking scare me like that again."

He gave a weak smile. "I'm still here, baby."

"I thought I lost you."

"I thought I was gone too," he admitted, pulling her into his good arm. "When I heard her yell my name, I ain't even have time to react. I just thought, *Fuck, I can't leave her. Not like this.*"

Tears welled in Dominique's eyes. "You didn't. You stayed."

"Shiiid, she only hit me in my shoulder. The other bullet grazed my side."

Dominique nestled herself carefully into the hospital bed beside Ramello, mindful of the bandage across his shoulder and the sling cradling his arm. The hospital room was dimly lit, quiet except for the gentle hum of machines and the muffled footsteps of night staff beyond the door. The soft buzz of the television provided background noise as she curled into his side, heart still fluttering with leftover adrenaline from the nightmare they'd just lived through.

Ramello looked over at her, exhaustion softening his sharp features. "You okay?"

"I should be asking you that," she whispered, fingers lightly brushing his jaw. "But… yeah. I think I am now."

He kissed her forehead. "You held me down."

Her eyes stung with tears. "I couldn't lose you. I meant what I said, Mello. You're all I got."

"I'm still here," he said gently. "I'm not goin' nowhere."

The volume on the TV rose slightly as the segment changed.

"Breaking news out of Miami International Airport," the anchor announced, voice cool and practiced. "Thirty-year-old Sierra Jones was arrested earlier today after opening fire inside the main terminal, injuring one passenger before being subdued by security."

Dominique froze.

They both turned toward the screen. A grainy video played, showing the chaotic airport footage: Sierra pushing through the crowd, the gun drawn. Ramello falling. People scattering. And then Sierra being tackled to the ground, still screaming.

The news cut to an officer speaking to reporters. "The suspect is currently in custody at Turner Guilford Knight Correctional Center where she is undergoing mental health evaluations. She is expected to be formally charged with attempted murder and multiple counts of reckless endangerment."

Dominique swallowed hard, her fingers tightening around Ramello's.

Then came the final blow.

It was a shaky clip of Sierra being escorted into the back of a police car, handcuffed, her hair a mess, eyes wild.

A reporter called out, "Sierra! Why did you do it?"

Sierra looked directly at the camera, her voice hoarse and unhinged. "She was mine… She was mine before he came around! He took her from me! She forgot who was really there for her. If he was gone, she'd come back…"

The screen flickered, switching to a commercial, but the silence it left behind was deafening.

Dominique was sick.

"She really lost it," Ramello murmured. "Like fully gone."

"She was already slipping," Dominique whispered. "But I never… I didn't think she'd go that far."

Ramello reached for her hand, linking their fingers. "I don't want you blamin' yourself. You tried with her. You did everything you could. But people break, and sometimes… they make choices that ain't got shit to do with you."

Dominique nodded, her lips trembling. "I know. It just hurts. I lost my best friend… and almost lost you."

"But you didn't." He kissed her knuckles. "I'm still here. And I'm not letting go."

She exhaled deeply, laying her head against his good shoulder. "I just want peace. I just want us."

He looked down at her with soft eyes then whispered, "That's all I want too."

They didn't speak again for a while. They didn't have to. Because even with the madness playing out just beyond the walls of that hospital room, in that moment, they had each other.

They were alive.

And they were free.

EPILOGUE

Three Weeks Later

THE CAR RIDE was quiet in the best kind of way. Dominique kept one hand on the wheel, the other resting over Ramello's thigh. He leaned back in the passenger seat, arm still in a sling, healing slowly but surely. The bruises were fading, but the fire in his eyes had never dulled.

Dominique's navigation system had her pull up to one of the most beautiful homes she had ever seen before.

Ramello stepped out and jogged around to open her door, offering his hand. She took it, still confused but intrigued, her sandals clicking lightly as they walked up the pristine driveway. The house stood tall. Modern yet warm with black iron accents, wide windows, and a sleek slate-gray exterior. There was a small garden out front already budding with flowers. The porch light was on, even though it was still bright out, like the house had been waiting for them.

She looked at him, one brow raised. "So, what is this?"

"Come see."

That was when Dominique noticed the beautiful, smiling realtor on the porch.

"Hello! You must be Dominique! I've heard so much

about you!" she greeted. "We've got y'all's final paperwork ready inside."

Dominique gasped softly the moment she stepped in.

The entryway opened into a sprawling living room with high ceilings and clean lines, flooded with natural light. Hardwood floors gleamed. The open-concept kitchen had marble counters, a chef's stove, and soft-close drawers that seemed to whisper wealth. Down the hall, she caught glimpses of multiple bedrooms, one clearly meant to be an office or creative space.

"Ramello…" Her voice dropped to a whisper. "What is this?"

"I looked at this spot right before we left for Miami," he said, coming up behind her and slipping his arms around her waist. "I been thinkin'. Your townhouse is cool. I love the energy in it… but we need space. For us. For what's next."

Her eyes widened, heart thudding. "You bought this?"

He smirked. "We're here to finish closing right now."

"You're really about to buy this house right now?"

He kissed her neck. "Yeah, baby. It's ours. And it's not just a home; it's an investment. Neighborhood's growing. Value gone triple in a few years. But more than all that…" He turned her to face him, so close she could feel his heartbeat.

"I needed to show you I'm serious about us. About building."

Dominique's lips parted, but she didn't know what to say. Her throat thickened.

"I been locked up, livin' day to day. Now, I'm finally free," he said, his voice low but steady. "And I don't ever wanna just survive again. I wanna live. I wanna build. And I wanna do that shit with you."

She swallowed hard as he pulled a small box from his pocket. Not a ring. Not yet. But inside was a delicate gold chain with a key charm hanging from it.

"I ain't proposin', not yet. But I am promisin'," he said, placing the necklace in her hand. "To love you. Protect you. Cherish you. No matter what. This house, this life, it's just the beginning. And if you say yes, we gone write the rest together."

Dominique stared at the key in her palm then up at him. Her eyes watered.

He had left her speechless.

They walked through the empty house, echoes of potential filling the high ceilings and sunlit rooms. Dominique grinned at the thought of decorating it, making it theirs.

Once everything was signed, the realtor tucked the documents away and chuckled. "Y'all sure picked a lot of space for just two people."

Dominique smiled slyly. "Actually..." She reached into her purse and pulled out a small box, handing it to Ramello.

He raised a brow and opened it. Inside were two positive pregnancy tests.

His mouth parted, stunned. He blinked down at them then up at her, eyes glossing. "You serious?"

Dominique nodded, tears threatening. "I found out just a couple of days ago. I wanted to wait 'til we were both breathing again. When we weren't so stressed, but... this moment couldn't be any more perfect."

Ramello wrapped his good arm around her, the other clutching the tests like treasure. "We makin' a whole life now," he whispered, voice thick with emotion. "Ain't nobody ever takin' that from us."

The realtor, misty-eyed herself, handed them a chilled bottle of champagne. "To new beginnings. And to love."

They thanked her and saw her out then stood alone in the empty kitchen, everything echoing around them.

"I meant what I said," Ramello told her, backing her

slowly against the counter. "I'm yours. Forever. Ain't no more prison."

She smiled, tears slipping free. "And I'm yours. Every piece of me."

He kissed her like he was learning her all over again, like she was a miracle he didn't deserve but got anyway. Clothes peeled off slowly, the champagne forgotten as they made love on the cold marble, their bodies warm and fused with gratitude.

The wounds Sierra left were still healing. The friendship Dominique once cherished had died the day Sierra chose hatred over love. And while Dominique would always mourn what they used to have… she would never forgive what she tried to take.

But love lived here now. And it wasn't going anywhere.

They had each other. A baby on the way. A house filled with dreams.

And no matter what came next… they'd choose each other. Every time.

The End

Did you enjoy the read?
Let us know how much by leaving us a
review on Amazon and Goodreads.

OTHER BOOKS BY

Urban Aint Dead

Tales 4rm Da Dale

The Hottest Summer Ever

Hittin' Licks For The Holidays: Atlanta

Wet Dreams On Lockdown: The Nurse

How To Publish A Book From Prison

How To Invest In The Stock Market From Prison

By **Elijah R. Freeman**

Despite The Odds

Despite The Odds 2

By **Juhnell Morgan**

Hittaz

Hittaz 2

Hittaz 3

Hittaz 4

Hittaz 5

Hittaz 6

Coldhearted

Coldhearted 2

Coldhearted 3

By **Lou Garden Price, Sr.**

Wizdom: Forever Your Gangsta

Charge It To The Game

Charge It To The Game 2

Charge It To The Game 3

A Summer To Remember With My Hitta

Snatched Up By A Hitta

Santa Sent Me A Real One For Christmas

Wet Dreams On Lockdown: The Unit Manager

Thug Me The Right Way 2

Thug Me The Right Way 3

Seizing A Gangsta's Heart For The Summer

Yours For The Taking

Wrapped Up In A Hitta's Love For Christmas

By **Nai**

A Set Up For Revenge

A Set Up For Revenge 2

Wet Dreams On Lockdown: The Librarian

By **Ashley Williams**

Trickin' On A Heaux For Christmas

Homie Hoppin' For The Holidays

Wet Dreams On Lockdown: The Female C.O

Letters Of His Love

By **Telia Teanna**

The State's Witness

The State's Witness 2

The State's Witness 3

This Time Won't You Save Me

This Time Won't You Save Me 2

His Summer Side Piece

A Holiday Heist

Healing The Heart Of A Detroit Gangsta

Summer Vows With A Detroit Gangsta

The Promissory

By **Kyiris Ashley**

Stuck In The Trenches

Stuck In The Trenches 2

By **Huff Tha Great**

Melted The Heart Of A Menace

Wet Dreams On Lockdown: Lieutenant Grace

By **P. Wise**

Merry Trapmas

By **Mia Sky**

Thug Me The Right Way

By **DiamondATL & Nai**

Wet Dreams On Lockdown: The Counselor

By **Paris Iman**

Wet Dreams On Lockdown: The Male C.O

By **Tamyra Griffin**

Wet Dreams On Lockdown: The Captain

By **TN Jones**

Wet Dreams On Lockdown: The Warden

By **Shawnice**

Atlantastan

Atlantastan 2

By **Chris Green**

IN The Streetz

IN The Streetz 2

IN The Streetz 3

IN The Streetz 4

IN The Streetz 5

By **Tron Hill**

Hittin' Licks For The Holidays: New York

Bandemic

By **Freshh Moneyy**

Coming Soon From
URBAN AINT DEAD

Drill
The Hottest Summer Ever 2
THE G-CODE
Tales 4rm Da Dale 2
How To Build Your Credit From Prison
By **Elijah R. Freeman**

Despite The Odds 3
By **Juhnell Morgan**

A YN'S Muse For The Summer
A Felon's Promise
By **Nai**

The Promissory 2
By **Kyiris Ashley**

Atlantastan 3
By **Chris Green**

IN The Streetz 6
By **Tron Hill**

Bandemic 2
By Freshh Moneyy

www.ingramcontent.com/pod-product-compliance
Lightning Source LLC
Chambersburg PA
CBHW071419300726
48976CB00004B/1171